# Winter's Walk

## MEL A ROWE

# Also by MEL A ROWE

Winter's Walk

The Football Whisperer

Avoiding the Pity Party

Unplanned Party


**THE ELSIE CREEK SERIES**

The ART of DUST

DIAMOND in the DUST

CAKED in DUST

XMAS DUST

# COPYRIGHT



**Caveat*: As a courtesy, there may be some sparse language choices in this story that may represent an obstacle for the reader and I am offering this warning. Please note this language is purely for fictional purposes only and not designed to offend any individual persons, culture, or religions implied.

## The Following Is Written In Australian English

# TABLE OF CONTENTS

Walking with a friend in the dark is
better than walking alone in the light

*Helen Keller*

# One

It was so beautiful and yet so dangerous. Among the ebony tiger stripes, gold shone like pineapple slices under a tropical sun. It was suited for an outback sunrise and warm red desert sands—not this patched stretch of country road. Yet, Jessica couldn't stop staring at it.

'OI.' Followed by a knock on her driver's window.

Jessica jumped, covering her lips to stop her screech at the man wearing a black beanie.

'Are you okay?' He asked.

Jessica nodded and wound down her window that allowed his spiced outdoor aroma of pure masculinity to fill her small car's interior. 'Fine,' she croaked, facing the road that rolled out like a dull grey carpet while her car remained obstructed.

'Tiger snake.' He stood tall, rubbing the snug fitting beanie on his head as if adjusting a baseball cap. With lips pursed, his dynamic denim eyes squinted at the snake that lay across the asphalt. 'Did you toot the horn?'

'Yes. But it wouldn't move.'

'How long have you been sitting there?' His sideways grin seemed to come easily.

Jessica shrugged.

'Most people would've run over it and checked their mirrors to see it hadn't flicked up into their axles.'

'Hey, being run over hurts, you know.' Her words were louder than intended.

'They're a protected species.'

'See,' she said, raising her chin higher, 'I was doing the right thing.'

'Stopping in the middle of the road?'

'He's spread out centre stage, not me.'

'You're the one blocking traffic.

'I'm protecting the wildlife.'

'It's sunbaking.'

'I noticed. But there's no way I'm leaving the safety of my seat when I have no idea how to shove off a snake.'

'*Yah!*' He stamped his boot and clapped his hands, chasing the snake into the yellow wildflowers that grew along the verge.

'You herded it like a cow.'

'Cow's don't bite.' Again, sharing that easy side grin, he gave a slight bow with a sweep of his hand that pointed toward the open road. 'You're free to go, please. Coz I can't pass when you're causing all this chaos to our peak hour traffic.'

Jessica looked back at his white ute loaded with lengths of timber. He was right. Her car was obstructing the deserted road slicing through farmlands waving new velvety growth of a future harvest.

Another car approached from behind, its driver called out, 'Everythin' all right, Brett?'

'Yeah, all good. It's just a sightseeing tourist causing a roadblock.' He thumbed at Jessica and asked her, 'Are you lost?'

Sure, he'd redefined the term of a working man's

rugged good looks with his tight long-sleeved t-shirt that outlined muscular arms that crossed over a well-toned chest. His flat waistline disappeared into the best set of thigh-hugging jeans on the planet—but he was rude.

Jessica had to look away, and engaged her car into gear. 'I know where I'm going.' And she had a deadline to meet.

'Aren't you gonna thank me for saving you?'

'What? You saved no one. All I was doing…' *Ugh*, he was right. She had been playing tourist, gawking at a snake spread out across the road. In her world, she'd never done that before. 'Thank you and good bye, Mr. Snake Charmer.' She drove off hoping the breeze would cool her flushed face.

'Snake charmer? I'm wearing a beanie, not a turban.'

Through the side-mirror she watched him lean down to the other car only to point back at her. *Great*, now the locals had someone new to talk about.

Why did she daydream while staring at a snake?

Because she'd hadn't been able to sleep going over her many mental checklists and time schedules for her escape to rural New South Wales.

Lush poplar trees framed Heart Springs' main street where shops on either side exuded a tasteful blend of a trendy café scene mixed with cottage crafts. The promise of homemade jams and warm bakeries made her tummy rumble, and the sweet scent of juicy plums displayed in the grocer's cart beckoned her.

Jessica spotted the Heart Springs' travel boutique and parked out front, smiling with hope at the store's posters showcasing a long-gone romantic era of mysterious exotic getaways.

This was her gateway to freedom, if only her damned leg would wake up.

With a fist, she thumped her numb left thigh and squeezed her toes in her shoes to get the blood flowing. The mechanical joints surrounding her knee shifted as she flexed her foot and was forced to bite down at the intense burst of pins and needles.

Even through the pain, it was still a good sign it worked.

She reached for her walking sticks, pulled herself out, and with laptop bag over her head and shoulders she stared at the storefront.

*Great—stairs. Where's the ramp? Hand rails?* Nothing but a set of over-sized front steps.

Jessica searched the sidewalk hoping for an easier access. Across the road it was only a slight step to enter the other shops. Except the pub that had a balcony she wouldn't visit in a hurry. But where the travel boutique stood, those shops were set higher above the curb.

'I can do this.' She had to.

Swallowing hard, she gripped her crutches. Gone was the full-leg restrictive brace. Now it was the Lofstrand elbow-crutches and a chunky half-leg caliper brace around the knee that always managed to catch on her clothes.

Jessica freed her long skirt from the brace, having dressed to impress for a reason. She blew at the stray strands that fell free from her top knot, and then shunted towards Heart Springs' Travel Boutique's door.

Each step made was another crucial step forward. She had their wish list and prayed they had hers.

# Two

'I made it.' Jessica beamed while allowing the door to bang shut behind her. She sipped her water bottle, delighted with herself for having conquered her mini-Everest. Even if it was performed in the most ungraceful manner of long and slow, she'd done it. Maybe she really could achieve her goal?

'Can I help you?' Asked the woman standing from behind her desk.

'Maggie Redmont?' Recognising the voice, Jessica

grinned at the woman with shoulder-length brown hair. Her rockabilly stylish skirt swung as if preparing to perform *Grease* on stage. With a wide smile and bright red lipstick, Maggie's look was fun and just what Jessica needed. 'Hi, I'm Jessica Pedersen, we spoke on the phone.'

'My website guru.' Maggie's infectious smile widened. 'Please come in. Did you climb those front steps?'

'Yes, I did.' Jessica grinned at accomplishing another challenge to her day. Yet, for some reason, climbing upwards was always easier than going down and she was not looking forward to that. 'You need a handrail out there.'

'Oh no, you're right,' Maggie said with a gasp. 'The amount of foot traffic I've lost because of our lousy entrance.'

'I wouldn't worry—'

'I do worry, because it's my business. I'd never thought of wheelchair access before.'

Jessica raised her chin higher. 'I don't have a wheelchair.' *Not anymore.*

'Please, have a seat.' With a rustle of her many skirts, Maggie walked and talked while looking outside her store's entrance. 'I understand now why you rented the Kimmel's cottage; it'll be perfect for you. It's got plenty of handrails and ramps.'

'It's not permanent.' Jessica refused to believe her injuries were lifelong.

'No, only six weeks. Here's the key.' Maggie placed a tagged brass key onto her desk. 'I'll draw you a mud map on how to get there. Now, Brett assures me you've got enough wood to last the next five winters.'

'Who?'

'Brett's your neighbour. He's super yummy to look at, but not much for conversation. He's one of the partners in the local gym. They're also glad you're here too.'

'But—I'm allergic to gyms, they fight against my chocolate addiction.' They reminded Jessica of rehab. A place of sterile surrounds and shiny machinery, being told what to do by people with perfect functioning limbs.

'When I bragged about my IT guru coming to remodel my website, they're hoping you'll do the same for them. Also, the crew at Tart's bakery and Bob's grill are keen, something about creating a takeout menu to order online. I think the pub wants you to update their site too? When you're done here, you should go and introduce yourself.'

'Wow. Really?' Jessica dropped into the visitor's chair and blinked up at Maggie. 'I mean, thank you.'

'It's a small town, hon, when talent arrives, we like to share, especially for the tourists.'

'Tourists, huh?' A name she'd been called twice today.

'I'm all about the tourist trade,' Maggie said, waving her hand around the boutique.

Admiring the vintage travel posters, Jessica was so glad she'd made the effort to come here in person. Now she had to convince Maggie of her request. 'Have you completed the brief?'

'Most of it.'

'We can schedule in a time—'

'First, let's get you settled. No dramas with the road trip?'

*Besides a sun-baking snake and a he-man boot-stomping wannabe hero.* 'No dramas.' Jessica giggled behind her fingertips that tapped against her lips. 'So, um, is my other trip booked?'

'Hey?' Maggie sat straighter behind her desk. 'Are you capable—'

'I can walk.' And getting better every day.

'Can you go hiking?'

'Maggie...' Jessica straightened out her skirt, correcting her posture. 'I'm here to do your website, and any other work available. I also want to use the walking tracks along the river and surrounding country roads to build up my endurance.' And to get away from her parents who wanted her strapped into a full-body armour of blankets to soften any blows from life.

'You can train in the city.'

'I don't need any witnesses until I've perfected my stride.'

'The Outback's a tough place.'

'I'm fully aware of that.'

'The Larapinta trail is a six day, hundred-kilometre hike. That doesn't sound easy to me.'

'I'm doing this for a reason. I need this, Maggie.' She held her breath in hope.

Maggie's chin lifted as her confident smile grew. 'Then you'll have the best time out there too. But I'll be checking to see if there are enough specialised provisions for you.' Maggie held up her palm to stop Jessica speaking. 'It's my job to ensure everything is available for my clients. Especially my IT guru.'

Jessica sighed with a smile. 'And that's why I came here for the excellent service.'

The door swung open and the breeze carried a familiar scent of spiced outdoors and masculinity that made Jessica's head turn.

'Oi, Maggie, got that wood you wanted for your shelves.'

'Hi, Brett, perfect timing.'

'Great, it's the snake charmer,' blurted out Jessica, as the heat rose as fast as her pulse. She blinked at the way the sun shone behind Brett through the open doorway, as if he were a gift from angels.

'Oi.' He frowned down at her.

'That's what you did?' Jessica couldn't help but stare at the tall tower of man with his wide muscular shoulders.

'Now that sounds like a story I want to hear.' Maggie snort-laughed at the pair and said, 'considering you're both new neighbours.'

'*What?*' Both Jessica and Brett gaped at Maggie, who shrugged from behind her desk.

'Did I miss something?' Maggie asked.

Brett pointed down at the seated Jessica. 'Only the

story of this one sitting in the centre of the road coz she couldn't be bothered getting out of the car—'

'Hey!' Jessica picked up her crutches and pushed herself upwards to face him. 'I did not want to run over that snake, okay. I told you, getting run over hurts like hell.'

'Aww, damn.' Brett hissed under his breath, his shoulders slumped, stepping away from her.

There it was, that pity look. Like she was some wounded thoroughbred destined to never leave the racetrack alive. Well, she wasn't beaten. Swiping the key and mud map from Maggie's desk, she said, 'We'll talk soon, Maggie.' Jessica gripped her elbow crutches with slow jerky movements and prepared herself for those oversized steps. Unfortunately, there were no more quick exits these days—which sucked.

'The back door's easier, Jessica.' Maggie scooted for the kitchenette in her peep-toe shoes. 'Brett, how fast can you make me a handrail for the front, and what about a ramp?'

Jessica followed Maggie through the office. 'Not for me?'

'You'll be my counsel for what my customers with

disabilities might need. Sorry, don't take offence,' Maggie said, pushing open the back door where sunlight streamed inside.

'I won't, and I'm not offended.' All prudish pride disappeared from daily pokes and prods by medical teams who never remembered her name. 'I'll be back tomorrow.'

'Can't wait.'

'How's the shop for food?' Should she shout herself a bottle of wine as a house warming celebration—or commiseration—for daring to do this on her own?

'I'm positive the stores have special parking right out front, and a ramp.'

It was a way of life few people noticed and they weren't expected to either. 'It's nice to meet you face to face, Maggie.' Even if she was the fool in front of Brett while being shown the backdoor.

'You too, Jessica.' Maggie reached over and hugged her.

'Wow, what a welcoming.' No client had ever done that before, she could almost melt on the spot. It was just what she needed.

'You wait and see. You're going to love it here.'

'Hope so.' If she avoided her neighbour these next

six weeks—no matter how good-looking he was—it'd be perfect.

Besides, men who looked like Brett never bothered with women like her. Jessica didn't need the pity, she needed to focus on completing her goals and had six weeks to do it.

Was she asking too much?

* * *

Maggie closed the back door with a thud as the swivel of her many skirts announced her return to the shop. 'Well, you put your foot into it, didn't you, Brett.'

*I'm an Idiot.* Brett hung his head. With measuring tape in hand, he hovered by the wall behind Maggie's desk. 'How was I supposed to know? She was sitting in her car in the middle of the road watching a snake.' He'd only stopped to see if she needed help. The woman with the warmest coffee-coloured eyes mixed with flecks of caramel stirred up the sweet tooth he didn't know he had until that fist sighting. What were the chances he'd see her again? 'Sorry to tick off your customer, Maggie.'

'You did worse than that, Brett.'

*Damn.* 'How?'

'That was my IT guru, who's also booked to update your gym's website.'

Brett groaned, rolling his eyes. Women were always organising things for him. Why couldn't they just leave him alone?

'I only came in to do a final measurement and to let you know I'll have your shelves ready tomorrow.' He should've stayed in the ute and gone home like he was supposed to. But no, he had to follow the mystery woman. So now he had to stick to his lame excuse. With tape in hand, pencil tucked behind his ear, he checked over his figures against the plans he'd spread over Maggie's desk.

'Brett, how fast can you do a set of handrails for those steps?' Maggie asked, pointing out the front windows.

'I'm not your wood-slave.' But he guessed who they were for.

The stranger who'd made a fool of him. And he deserved it too.

Normally he'd avoid conversation with most people—all people in general if he could. Yet he'd seen her sitting in the car, with those warm eyes and lush red lips hidden behind tapping fingertips. 'How long is she staying, Maggie?' Why was he even bothering to ask? The woman probably hated him?

'As long as it takes to update my website, and…' Maggie turned with a swoosh of those skirts. 'She's here to train.'

'For what?'

'You've trekked the Kokoda trail?'

'With some of my mates. Jessica's not—' He turned around to face Maggie's cheesy grin.

'Jessica's doing the Larapinta trail.'

'Where's that?'

'It starts in Alice Springs and goes right through the red centre.'

'Do they have facilities for people like Jessica?' Why would a woman in Jessica's situation go hiking in the outback? She was flat out doing a set of front steps into Maggie's store, how the hell was Jessica going to hike a mountain range! She was either pretty gutsy, stupid, or purposely setting herself up to fail for the attention.

Maggie sat at her desk and started tapping away at the keyboard. 'Can you offer Jessica any tips?'

'For what?'

'Besides snake charming, how about sharing some hiking tips.'

'Yeah, tell her to go to the gym where the crew can look after her there.' Coz Brett didn't want to talk to anyone.

'Jessica doesn't like gyms.'

'And that makes two of us.' He folded up his sketched plans and wound up his measuring tape with a recoiling click.

'Why own a gym when you don't like it, Brett?'

He scowled, opening the door. 'Because it was never my choice.'

# Three

Jessica pushed open the creaking back door and checked the cottage's wooden floors for any slippery rugs as she shuffled inside.

She sighed with frustration at how much easier it used to be to unpack her car, letting the shopping bags slide off her reddened forearms and onto the kitchen counter. The simple wooden top was the perfect leaning height for her, where everything was within reach. It'd make cooking so much easier. *Thank you, Mrs Kimmel.*

There was a massive fireplace that was the centrepiece of the large open plan room, with a comfy couch and overstuffed armchairs that were perfect for reading. She could just picture her Sunday-plan coming to fruition of actually reading a fiction book while glancing at the emerald fields peppered with grazing cattle.

But it was all too quiet.

No cars drove past. There were no neighbourhood noises. No aromas of meals being cooked. No household sounds of Mum telling Dad to turn down the TV which bellowed out the latest sadness in the world.

The open lush fields only reminded her that there were no more Sunday golf sessions. The weekly family ritual of teaming up with her brother, where they'd share alibis to face the fairway together to play with their parents. They used to regularly swap secrets of their late-night adventures along the back nine, but now, her brother avoided her like the plague.

Jessica also avoided all outdoor functions if she could. Especially the ones with family friends' expressions of shameful horror if she fell down while perfecting her step, let alone trying to improve her swing. Why play a sport when she was flat out walking a set of stairs and had a car to unpack that might take her until midnight.

The wind rattled the windows as the back door swung open hitting the wall with a bang. She jumped with fright, clutching the stone walls to keep her balance.

She swallowed down the fear that started to claw upwards from her belly at the realisation that she was all alone surrounded by nothing but countryside. She'd never done country. Ever.

What possessed her to make such a bold move?

'I'm doing this because it's all part of the plan.' And slammed the backdoor shut.

Jessica dragged herself further into the kitchen. She leaned her right hip against the stone bench-side. Its coolness pressed though her skirt as she lifted the hem to expose her leg brace. She unclipped its fast release latches and sighed with pure relief as she dumped the corset-styled contraption onto the bench. At least the rigid metal rods had been replaced by flexible pieces hidden within the brace that were so much smaller and lighter the more time passed since the accident.

The day that had unleashed hell.

Now, truly standing on her own two feet, she

grinned wide. 'I'm home alone.' If she could dance, she would.

With her hand caressing the smooth stone walls, she explored the small cottage she was going to call home for the next six weeks. It wasn't too long a time to settle in, but it was enough time to prove to her family and herself she was ready to return to her place in the world. Wherever that may be?

She lay back on the huge bed, gazing at the amazing view of the countryside through the bedside wall of windows. Exhausted, she was tempted to lay there for the rest of the day, but forced herself to discover more.

'Aww.' Her voice echoed in the spacious bathroom as she smiled at the hand rails surrounding the magnificent tub with the best view of the country side.

It was nothing like her parents' place where she'd been confined to showers, seated in a chair. Her mum guarded the cubicle in case she fell while her dad cringed in the corridor for back-up. They needed this break as much as she did.

In the lounge room, Jessica pushed the large wooden table to the centre of the room. This would be her office with a glorious view of the gentle cascading countryside to be accompanied by the crackling warmth of a fire place—once she'd worked out how to use it.

With her desk now in the perfect position to set up all her equipment, she hobbled over to the kitchen bench. Ravenous, and eager to cook for herself again, she unpacked her groceries.

Noting the time, she knew she'd have to check in with her parents soon, that was the deal.

Jessica loved the dynamic couple. She also wanted her independence back. To return to work, and move out of her childhood home, the way it used to be.

Of course, it'd never be the same.

Not since she'd been run over and kicked kerbside like a dead dog on the side of the road.

Already moving in the right direction, she limped toward her car and stopped to stare at the flame red streaks that slashed across the darkening skyline. She wanted to shout out to someone to share this scene with her. But there was no one.

She wasn't scared of being alone. She'd pretty much accepted being single the day she'd woken up and was informed of her body's damage as the doctors explained her lifestyle changes. It wasn't just her hip, but her whole world had been shattered along with her soul.

But that was all about to change.

# Four

Sunrise had yet to start its stretch across the horizon as dew dripped from the cottage's corrugated roof. Jessica stepped out in her hiking boots. Her crutches had been replaced for a pair of lightweight trekking poles.

She struggled with her backpack's loose shoulder straps as she hunched over from its shifting weight.

One step after the other, dirt and stones crunched under her boots as she faced the dark driveway. She drove her poles into the dirt, then she watched her leg slide forward. Head up, she looked to the path ahead, then back down at the ground and slid her leg forward.

With the thick soles, her step was unsure on the gravel and the boot's laces were so tight her toes tingled from lack of circulation. The heavy backpack dug into her lower back, while her beanie kept sliding down to block her view, and her grip slipped on the tall trekking poles.

But still, she kept going.

A kangaroo leaped across her path. She screamed and jumped back, losing her balance as her leg gave way and she landed on her back like a turtle. All while the kangaroo jumped the fence and bounded away.

'*Great.*' Jessica groaned and huffed and puffed in the many layers of clothing. First too cold, now too hot, and… stuffed.

She stared at the light she'd left on at the cottage. She hadn't even made it to the main road yet.

A low engine rumbled and the slash of headlights travelled down the dirt track from behind.

Who was coming to share in her shame now? Surely it was too early, even for farmers.

'Morning,' called out Brett from the open driver's window as he stopped his ute and peered at Jessica lying in the wild grass.

'Typical.' Of all the people who had to witness her wallow in the wilderness it had to be Brett.

'Need a hand?'

'I've got this.' She tried to roll from side to side, but her backpack wouldn't budge. Instead, she unclipped it, slid out of the shoulder straps, and sat upright. 'Nothing to see here.'

'Ah huh.'

*Stuff his smug expression.* 'No snakes here, so you might want to keep moving or you'll be the next one accused of stopping traffic.' She hoped there were no snakes?

'It's my lane and I can stop here if I want to. We share this track. My place is over the hill.' Brett jumped out of his cab, picked up her trekking poles, and then held out his hand to her. 'Come on.'

She frowned up at him. 'I said—'

'Your arse is getting wet sitting in the dew.' Then he pulled her upright before she had a chance to react.

'Hey, I can do this.' How strong was he to pluck her off the ground so effortlessly? Inhaling his fresh soap and shampooed hair tickled her tastebuds. They were so close his body heat only added to her overburdened internal thermostat.

'Sure, you can. But these poles are too high for you. Didn't they measure you up?'

'I bought them online.'

Brett lined up the lightweight trekking poles against her frame, lowered them a few rungs and then held them out to her. 'How's that?'

Jessica reached for the handles trying to avoid touching his strong hands. 'Okay, I guess.' Another flush of heat crept up her neck for forgetting the basics on making adjustments. She would've worked it out. Eventually.

Brett scooped her pack up by the straps. 'This is too heavy. What have you got in here?'

'Bricks.' She pressed tingling fingertips against her lips to stop the drool escaping at the way his biceps bulged from doing an arm curl with her weighty pack.

'You're supposed to start small and then add to it,' Brett said, pulling out four bricks from her backpack that he tossed into the rear tray of his ute.

Now he was being rude again. 'What do you care?' Hello, they were strangers in the dark arguing before dawn, which was so not part of her normal routine. But she'd planned to walk early before she sat at her desk for the day.

'I heard you're attempting to do the Larapinta trek.'

The brute who smelled way too good, and was hotter than a noonday summer sun, seemed to know what he was doing with her equipment. 'Have you done that trek?

'No. I did Kokoda.'

'Wow, that's hard core. Larapinta's only medium grade.' See, she'd done her research.

'Have you ever hiked before?' Brett asked, holding out her pack to her back and shoulders.

'I'm learning.' It was all part of her re-learning how to walk programme.

Her teeth snagged her bottom lip as he slid the straps over her shoulders, then he stood in front of her making more adjustments to her pack.

'Are you a walking sauna, too?'

'Well, I'm not gonna wear a ball-gown and stilettos to go jump country fences in winter, now am I?' No, she was supposed to be breaking a sweat free from witnesses.

The laugh lines crinkled around his eyes as he gave a zip-tight tug on the straps on her shoulders that snapped her spine straight, then he clipped up the waist band.

She felt like a baby strapped into a car seat.

'I don't need help. Okay? And I certainly don't need you to babysit me.' Not like her parents did, ever since she'd been let out of hospital.

'I'm not babysitting, I'm only adjusting your gear to suit your body-build before you ruin it.'

'Um, thanks.' Why did he make her so flustered? And were those straps too tight that it was making it hard to breathe?

Brett squinted those denim eyes at her as he adjusted his beanie. 'So, you're out here to use this place as a training camp?'

'It's not a prison camp,' she said, pushing away from his solid wall of muscle and shuffling onto the track. 'Is this a country neighbourly-interfering thing you're doing?'

'Don't worry, I won't be in your face. I like my privacy.' In a few long-legged strides, Brett returned to his ute's driver's seat. The cab's door creaked shut, and he rested his elbow on the open window frame. 'There are easier walking tracks in town you should try first. You'll need to walk long distances if you're thinking of hiking for six days. It's obvious you've got the upper arm strength from using crutches, but…'

She scowled at him.

'You'll need to focus more on your legs.' Brett continued, tilting his head as his eyes scanned over her entire body.

Even with layers of leggings, cargo pants, and a lumpy leg brace on, she still felt naked under his stare. 'I'm trying.'

'The way those boots are laced they'll give you blisters and cut off the circulation in your toes in no time.'

Were there tricks to lacing up shoes no one told her about? 'But—'

'You look like you're running a cross-country skiing marathon without snow. Why are you putting yourself through all of this?'

Jessica straightened as she raised her chin. 'Because I can.'

She speared her pole-tips into the soft dirt and shunted forwards. She didn't need anyone's charity.

Especially not from her bantering body-beautiful neighbour, when she hadn't even had her first coffee yet.

* * *

Brett shook his head at Jessica's determination and that stubborn streak forcing those hiking poles into the ground. He had to admire her spirit because few able-bodied people would bother.

Still, it bothered him.

Normally he'd never interfere, but she was handicapped, not only by her physical impairment, it was also pretty damned obvious she'd never lived in the country, based on her clothing to trek a country lane without a torch. In the dark.

He was so close to bundling her up to drag her back to Kimmel's cottage and put her down in front of a warm fire—not leave her out here to stumble in the dark, alone.

Brett couldn't go through that again, not another woman getting sick on him.

Yet, he was all thumbs when it came to talking to Jessica. What the heck were the politically correct terminologies to use for her condition?

Was he that out of practise to not know how to hold a conversation?

But he knew what he was talking about when it came to her hiking gear. He'd trekked Kokoda, where he'd trained for months alongside his mad mate Mick. They'd done it together to help cope with losing their other mates, where those ghosts still whispered in his ear.

Tucking the beanie over his ears, he put the ute into gear. He hated opening the gym in the mornings, but it was a part of a life he hadn't let go of, because he didn't know how.

Glancing through the rear-view mirror, he shook his head at Jessica's hiking technique. That irritating woman was going to cause herself a whole lot of aches and pains with her posture alone.

He doubted she'd make it to the weekend.

# Five

Stale sweat and assorted deodorants churned in the air-conditioning as music videos flashed from the big screen that accompanied the up-tempo beat. Jessica sighed with envy at the woman pounding miles on a treadmill.

Although proud, she'd managed to complete day two of her self-torture tour and for making it half-way down the shared track towards the main road. But with blisters and shoulder stress, her progress had been slow. Was she doing it wrong?

She didn't dare ask the neighbour for advice,

preferring to wait until Brett drove past to start her morning walk. She couldn't picture Brett, the rugged working man in his perfect grease-stained jeans, boots, and work shirts, as the owner of a gym. Did Brett even own anything spandex? Let alone sweatshirts, or sneakers?

Brett didn't need to workout, not when he had outdoors work. Like how he'd fixed the potholes in their shared driveway, without a shirt on. She couldn't stop staring at his tanned, toned torso long after her cup of tea went cold.

But she was here now, because Maggie had made this appointment. It seemed word had spread with Jessica getting daily queries for work. Heart Springs was proving to be a gold mine for her small business.

'Can I help you?' Asked the woman in a mega-toned body, bouncing on the balls of her feet.

'Are you the manager?'

'No, I'm Kelly.'

'I've got an appointment with the manager.' *Please don't let it be Brett.*

'This way.' Kelly led with a bounce, as Jessica shunted behind her. 'Nicole, our new client's here,' Kelly shouted at the open office doorway.

'I'm not a client.'

'Are you sure?'

'I have my own routine.' Which was killing herself at dawn, and she'd never slept better.

Jessica entered the office filled with cartons of assorted drink bottles where a woman was focusing on a paperwork covered desk. 'Hi, I'm Jessica, I'm here to help with your website.'

'Welcome, I'm Nicole. Care for a drink?' Nicole waved at the boxes of bottled sports drinks as she arose from her desk that faced the wall.

'I'm okay, thanks.' Jessica shuffled to the offered chair and smiled at Nicole's open warmth.

'You look okay, too.'

Strange for someone she'd just met to say such a thing.

'Maggie called.'

'I see.' Magical-Maggie wasn't only a brilliant travel agent, she was fast becoming Jessica's BFF. 'Did you complete the emailed brief?'

'I've been waiting for Brett's opinion.'

'Your partner?'

'Business partner. My husband and I bought this

place with our daughter Fiona, and her husband Brett. This is Fiona on their wedding day.' Nicole passed a framed photo of Brett standing beside a beautiful blonde bride.

'I haven't met Fiona.' *Of course, he was married.* She could just kick herself for perving on a married man.

'She died.'

Jessica's stomach dropped for Nicole, but mostly for Brett. 'I'm so sorry.'

'Me too.' Nicole sighed, returning the frame to her desk. 'This was Fiona's dream of helping people to become healthier, yet ended up sick herself.'

Jessica hugged her laptop bag closer, unsure of what to say.

'Maggie tells me you're staying at the Kimmel's cottage.'

'I am, for six weeks.'

'Then off to do the Larapinta trail. That's such an exciting goal. You should speak with Brett, he did Kokoda soon after Fiona passed. We were expecting him to reenlist after that, but he chose to stay. I'll call Brett to return to town,' Nicole said, picking up the phone. 'If Brett didn't open the gym in the mornings, I doubt we'd ever see him leave that farm of his, so this'll be a bonus.'

Jessica wanted to ask what happened to Fiona, reminding her that there was always someone in a worse state than her. It was a part of her mantra that kept her going, replaying over and over that she was still alive, still breathing, and walking better every single day. Maybe she should make time to do another practise walk for lunch? 'I can return another time.'

'Brett won't be long''

'Great.' *Not.*

'We can at least make a start until he gets here.'

'That we can.' Grateful for the new clients, Jessica slid her chair closer and pulled out her laptop. Her fingertips itched to play because she didn't need legs to dance across the keyboard. This was the part of her that just got stronger, and she loved it.

The gym door swung open and Brett's boots clomped along the floorboards as the loud music masked the grunts and groans of those sweating in air-conditioning.

'Good morning, Brett, how are you today?' Kelly asked with a wide smile as she waved enthusiastically from behind the counter, like a window-cleaner on speed.

'Only saw you two hours ago, Kelly, nothing's changed.' He walked past the gym instructor who practically lived here, and into the office, heading straight for the coffee pot. 'You rang, Nic?'

'You've met Jessica.'

With cup halfway to his mouth, he stopped to stare over the steam at Jessica seated at the desk with the perfect posture of an Olympic equestrian rider. Her rich milk chocolate hair twirled into a knot on top of her head defied gravity, with its soft stray curls that fell around her slender neck to frame her delicate facial features. She peered at him through honey-framed glasses that highlighted the caramel in those coffee-coloured eyes The woman was stunning, and he drank deep from his cup to quench the dryness of his mouth.

'We've met.' Jessica gave him a curt nod before turning back to the screen.

'What do you want?' He ignored Nicole's frown for his uncivil behaviour towards the beauty who only brought out his inner beast. He was always getting tongue-tied around Jessica—*why?*

'Jessica's making over our website, remember?'

'Well, you don't need me then.' Putting his cup down he made his move to escape.

'Yes, we do,' said Nicole, pointing to the spare chair.

'Why isn't Bob here?'

'He's gone fishing.'

'Where's my invite?'

'Bob gave up asking because you always say no.'

'I had pot holes to fix.' And new neighbours to avoid.

'Always an excuse. Now sit, young man.'

Brett winced as he rubbed his beanie on his head. He had no choice, so he sat down, crossed his leg over his knee and reached for his coffee. 'What do I have to do?' He asked, taking sneaky glances at Jessica powering over the office keyboard like a wizard.

'We answer these questions for Jessica.'

'Hold on, what qualifications does Jessica have to access our website? There's sensitive material on our system.' Brett flinched internally as Jessica's tapdancing fingers stopped to hover over the keypad and she turned to face him.

'I did my IT internship with the government,

managing their websites. I've worked with lots of highly sensitive data and I'll gladly sign any confidentiality agreement you have available. Besides, I'm not bored enough to hack into your personal porn collection.'

'Oi.' *Not in front of the mother-in-law.* He glared at Jessica, who was again staring at the monitor, tapping her fingertips across lush full lips. Even annoyed with her, he wanted those eyes on him just to drink in the view.

'Okay then.' Nicole patted Brett on the knee and turned to Jessica asking, 'What questions do you have?'

'Besides an obvious upgrade, what is your site's main purpose?'

'To advertise in hope of catching the odd tourist or two,' replied Nicole. 'The locals know us from word of mouth, but we need to be more accessible to visitors who come to stay.'

'Word of mouth is great in this small town. I haven't been here a week and there's work lined up for me, when I've only spoken to Maggie.'

'And me,' said Brett, not that he'd call it a conversation.

'Do I have you to thank for the extra business I'm

getting?' Jessica asked, glancing at him sideways through her glasses.

*Finally*, she looked at him.

'Me, no. I, ah, don't talk to anyone,' he blurted out, and caught Nicole's frown. *Damn.* From that look, he was going to suffer daily visits of mothering for the rest of the week. 'How's your trek-training going?'

'Okay,' mumbled Jessica with her head down as the colour creeped into her fair cheeks.

'How are you training?' Nicole asked Jessica.

'Jessica's walking the lane in the mornings.'

'Are you helping her, Brett?'

'NO,' Jessica and Brett said together, glaring at each other.

'I don't need help,' Jessica said.

'Hey, hold on a sec—' He sat forward, facing the stubborn female. 'I didn't offer. And I'm busy.'

'I'm fine doing what I got told.'

'Who told you to carry ten bricks in an unsecured backpack? Lemme guess, it was the same place you got those poles from.'

Jessica shrugged and faced the computer screen

'Do you have someone helping you, Jessica?' Nicole asked.

'I have a plan from my—'

'Not some random online guru's plan for the masses,' butted in Brett with a frown, leaning back in his seat.

Jessica turned fast, scowling at him 'Hey, do I interfere with your business?'

'Yes, you're doing our website.'

'Do I need to split you two up or do I put you both into a boxing ring?' Nicole asked, eyeing off the pair.

'Jessica could do with the hand and leg combination workout.' Brett cocked his head and gazed over her slender figure. He wouldn't want her muscle-bound, not when she was perfectly proportioned with her soft feminine curves.

'Leave me alone, I'm only here to help. Maybe, I should go,' Jessica said, reaching for her crutches.

Nicole placed her palm on Jessica's shoulder. 'No, don't. We need this site. Brett, behave. It's not Jessica's fault you hate change and don't want to be here.'

Brett grunted, frowning at the female duo. *Women.* He couldn't go against them if he tried. He'd learned long ago, when they ganged up on him like this, it was either walk away or sit silently and take it like a man. So, he shut up and waited for them to forget he was even in the room.

*  *  *

Jessica couldn't concentrate in Brett's presence. She could feel him watching her, while his scent of rugged masculine outdoors tickled her nose. Normally, she dealt with customers by phone or email, where house calls never happened.

But she wanted to be different to any other IT person out there. Jessica wanted to offer a unique customised service as part of her business plan. And that started by doing onsite visits, to gain a better understanding of her clients' needs and their personalities. Then she could go back to being the voice over the phone while working in her socks and jammies at home.

She could do this gig with her eyes closed—but not with Brett in the room. He was everywhere.

'Okay, fine, do the site.' He tore off his beanie and raked fingers through his short hair that was the colour of cinnamon and cedar. It perfectly capped of his masculine features. Dark facial growth shaded his cheekbones and strong jaw-line like a charcoal sketch destined for museum walls. Trapped by his gaze, she struggled to breathe the same airspace. *Not good.*

She pinched her thigh, turned to the screen, pushed up her glasses, and tapped her fingertips across her lips. *Focus.* 'I'll at least do a search on your site's metadata to add some keywords to improve your SEO. What other features would you like?'

'I'm not sure,' Nicole said. 'What do other people have?'

'Class times, upcoming events, seasonal specials, that sort of thing. I've created a list of the highest-ranking gym websites for you. See what appeals to you and answer the questionnaire. When you're ready, call or email me and we can set up another time.' Jessica gave an exaggerated flourish on the keyboard like a concert pianist in a symphony battle-off. She slid her laptop into her workbag. Gave a tight smile to Nicole and a stern nod to Brett. Trying to control her hand tremor, she left her business card on the desk, then scooped up her crutches and headed for the exit. Fast.

'You're leaving already,' complained Brett.

'Decide what you want, and when you've finished,

call me. It's no rush. I'm flexible.'

'Yeah, right.'

'Brett.' Nicole slapped Brett's denim-clad thigh.

'I didn't mean her handicap thing, I was—'

'*Brett.*' Nicole glared at him. 'I'm so sorry, Jessica.'

'It's okay. Nice to meet you, Nicole.' Gripping her crutches tightly as the caliper's joints around her knee somehow tripled in its weight. Yet, she remained calm, even though his words stung. Handicap. Invalid. Words regularly thrown in her face. Unable to meet their eyes and with hunched shoulders, she shunted out the door as fast as she could.

Brett dropped his head to his chest. *I'm such an idiot.* 'Don't say it Nic, I know I'm an arsehole.' Dodging the death stare from his other-mother, Brett chased after Jessica.

'Hey, Jess?' He cocked his eyebrow at how fast she hiked in those crutches toward her sedan. It was impressive. Why didn't she park in the accessible space clearly marked by the front door? 'Jess, I'm sorry. I didn't mean it to sound like that.'

'Go away.'

'Let me help.' He reached for the driver's door.

'I don't need your help.' She shoved him aside, then threw her crutches onto the passenger seat.

'I'm sorry.'

'For what, upsetting the cripple? If I wasn't crippled would you still give me grief?'

'Yes. No. I dunno?' He stepped back, raking fingers through his hair. 'Why do you confuse the hell out me?'

'What?'

He was sucker-punched at the depth of sorrow in her eyes. *Idiot*. 'Sorry, okay. Look, I've got best mates missing limbs and I'm fine around them, but you—'

'I'm not made of glass, I may be broken but I don't shatter that easy,' she said with a lowered tone as she slid into her front seat.

'What the—' He stopped all movement at the flash of her creamy thighs while she fought with her skirt caught in the leg brace. Long, soft, supple legs that no doubt led to paradise. *Damn*. He rubbed his forehead to focus as he stepped back.

'I'm, ah, trying to apologise,' he stuttered, inhaling her invisible wave of heavenly sweetness.

'No need, Snake Charmer. Go find something else that slithers to scare away.' She slammed the door shut and soon drove away.

Brett watched until her car disappeared, then turned towards the gym where Nicole was waiting for him at the doorway.

'Why did you leave me with this, Fiona?' Brett whispered to the grey sky, then plonked his beanie back on. He didn't need the drama.

But if he didn't deal with Nicole now, she'd follow him home. *Women.* He only talked to the few he'd grown up with, who were so familiar to his landscape he never saw them.

What made Jessica so different?

# Six

Jessica gloved up and opened the back door to be greeted by a blast of pre-dawn icy air that stung her cheeks. Lowering her beanie over her ears, she raised her scarf to cover her lips. Was she going to be warm enough?

With the height of winter almost here, she was tempted to stoke up the fireplace and crawl under a dozen blankets to spend the rest of the day in bed.

Instead, she locked the door, hitched her pack to find that sweet nestling spot on her spine. She gripped her hiking poles and was soon swallowed in the darkness as the moon peeked past slow-moving clouds that dotted the darkened skyline.

The only sound was the gravel crunching beneath her boots on the driveway. The aroma of the rich earth was invigorating, but the silhouettes of the trees were unnerving.

She dodged the fresh-filled potholes on the shared track and turned right towards the main road. Never left to Brett's place that was hidden behind the small rise where the glow of lights hinted at his existence.

'You should have a torch with you.'

'AUUUUGGHH!' Her scream echoed as she jumped back, her leg crumpled, and in a flash, Brett grabbed her arms and held her upright.

'I'm sure our other neighbours heard you.'

'Brett?' Her heart almost burst out of her chest, licking her dry lips at the man who'd been crashing her dreams. 'What are you doing here?'

'Here's a torch.' He plonked the headlamp's elastic band over her beanie, pushing it down it blinded her.

She tore off the beanie. 'Wh-what?'

'Can't you speak clearly this early in the—'

'STOP.' She raised her hand at him like a traffic sign as her words echoed into the darkness. 'Why are you here?'

'To help.'

'Why?'

'Because I was an arsehole yesterday after what I'd said, and…'

She tilted her head, squinting at him. 'The whole truth.'

'Okay.' Brett sighed and rubbed at his beanie on his head. 'I had Nic on my back for being rude to you, and—'

'Do you have nits?'

'What?'

'The way you're always scratching your head as part of your thought process?'

'No.' He went to scratch his head and frowned at her grin. 'Do you?'

'No. Although talking about it makes me itch.' She giggled, scratching her scalp, slipping on her own beanie and adjusted the headlamp he'd given her. 'If you're feeling so guilty why scare the daylight out of me?' She turned her back on him and shuffled along the track, she had a schedule to keep. 'Thanks for the torch it's a nice touch.'

'You're welcome,' replied Brett as he stepped in beside her.

She frowned at his long stride that was one to her two-and-a-half steps.

'Stop staring at the dirt and watch the path ahead.'

'Excuse me?'

'The torch will light the way if you didn't look down all the time.'

'I do not.'

'You do too.'

How long had he been watching her? 'I...I...' She sighed, watching her boots shuffle across the dirt. 'I don't want to fall?'

'What happens if you do?'

She bit her lip, gripping her poles tighter, and just kept on walking.

'It's not a trick question. You told me you weren't made of glass yesterday, or are you worried you'll hurt yourself?'

'Nothing worse than what I've been through.'

'So, you're still adjusting?'

Hiding her wince, she shrugged, too embarrassed to talk. Not that they were talking.

'So, if you fall, you'd pick yourself up, right?'

She tried to, and gave him a nod.

'Your feet know what they're doing, right?'

'Most of the time.'

'You said it hurts to get run over—'

*Duh!* 'It does when you end up with a crushed pelvis and nerve damage.'

'Meaning?'

She gave a heavy sigh and explained in the monotone of a well-rehearsed speech. 'Femoral nerve damage impairs movement and creates a loss of sensation in the thigh muscle, it's weakened that leg. Sometimes it won't straighten and I don't trust it because it collapses on me.'

'Which is why you have the brace?'

'Yes, Doctor Do-good. Any more questions before dawn?'

His slow side-grin grew and it looked better than the sunrise. *Not good.*

Brett strolled with hands in his jean's pockets, watching her stride. 'So, your lower leg and foot are okay?'

'Yes, but there's this gap that mixes messages for movement. But I'm getting better.'

'I get it. So, because you're worried it won't work, instead of trusting it, you look at the ground getting ready for it to break.'

'Are you a physio or something?'

'No. What happens if you trusted your body to hold you and move like it's always done? So what if you fall.' He walked ahead of her on the track, saying, 'You'll pick yourself up, dust yourself off, and keep on walking.'

'Go away, I don't need a personal trainer.' Distance was good and shuffled onwards even if it was impossible to pass the guy in his perfect thigh-hugging jeans.

'But I can help you.'

'I don't need it.'

'Fine, I'm just walking my track on my land.'

'You don't have to do it this time of the morning.'

'How do you know this isn't my normal time to check out my track, but instead, I've been avoiding you?'

Which is exactly what she'd been doing, as the heated flush prickled in her cheeks. *Smart arse.* 'I thought you opened the gym?'

'Nic's got Kelly doing it a few times during the week for yoga classes.'

'Kelly's a yoga instructor?' Was she his girlfriend too?

'That and a personal trainer, and the bouncer.' He chuckled, springing up and down on his toes.

'I noticed.' Giggling at his antics.

'So you do smile.'

'I smile,' she said, frowning again. 'You don't need to do this.'

'I know.'

'You can go.'

'I could.'

'Why are you still here?'

'Because I am. Can I ask you something?'

'Do I have any choice?' He owned the track so she couldn't shake him.

'Why are you doing the Larapinta trail? Why train here and not where you're from?'

'Because,' focusing on her steps, anywhere but looking at Brett, she admitted, 'my family wouldn't let me.'

'Why not?'

'They haven't let me do anything for myself, not since…' She looked away. Why was she babbling all her secrets to him?

'So this condition is only recent?'

'Almost a year ago.'

'What happened?'

'Hit and run. All I remember is I'd finished work and somehow this van cleaned me up in the office car park.' She was used to the many questions from the police, the rehab staff, her mum, her mum's friends…

'Did you quit that job?'

Jessica shrugged. 'I hated where they had me and didn't have the heart to return. And,' she swallowed and croaked to the guy who didn't like change, 'I needed a change.'

'Your whole world would've changed.'

Few people realised how dramatic it had been for her.

'Do you think they'd treat you differently at work because of your physical limitations?'

'Swallow the disabled persons' dictionary, did we?' Her smirk was matched by Brett's easy side-smile.

'I rang my mate last night, we served together as combat engineers.'

'Sounds like a dangerous job?'

'It had its moment. Mick lost his leg from a landmine.'

'Where were you?' She stopped in her tracks with

her heart hitching she almost reached out to hold his arm. But didn't.

'I was here, with Fiona while she…' This time it was Brett's turn to falter, clearing his throat to stare at the silent countryside surrounding them.

'I'm sorry about your wife,' Jessica said with steam coming off her breath that disappeared into the chilly air. She resumed her shuffle down the track, noting Brett never wore a wedding band.

'Me too.' He shrugged as he adjusted his beanie and caught her grin. 'I don't have nits. It's a habit. The same as you tap your lips with your fingertips like you're playing the piano.'

She stopped and stared at him.

'Have I ticked you off again?'

'You irritate me,' she blurted out truthfully, taking a step ahead.

He stopped and grabbed her arm. 'I'm trying—'

'I'll say.'

'You're not helping.' He sniffed and looked down the dark track as if trying to find his patience while she shuffled past. 'Okay, I'll tell you something I've never told a soul.'

'I don't need to know your secrets.'

'It might help.'

'Help why, when you're leaving?'

'I've forgotten how to talk to people.'

'You talk to people.'

He stopped and said in a commanding voice, 'I've forgotten how to have a conversation with new people, because ever since Fiona died, I found it easier to avoid people in general.'

That killed her inner fight.

Jessica continued with her dirt-shuffle down the track. 'Nicole said if you didn't open the gym in the morning, you'd never leave the farm.'

Again, he stepped in beside her. 'That's true, I love it here. Do you hide behind your screens? Look up.'

Jessica frowned because Brett was right. She looked towards the track, illuminated by the glow of her headlamp.

Fair's fair, Brett was trying. She couldn't hate him for it, when she could relate. 'Most of my conversations are via phone or Skype and no site visits. No one sees what's under the table and they take me for my intellectual skills and not the physical.'

'Are you ashamed of yourself?'

'I don't want their pity.'

'Anyone here in town treat you like that?'

'You did.'

Brett winced. 'Look, I'm sorry for what I'd said in front of Maggie, and Nic, and...'

'Apology accepted. Now, thank you for the offer, but I don't need your help.'

'Yeah you do, and I'm trying to hold a conversation.'

*Oh man, why?* She rolled her eyes at the awakening skyline.

'How come you aren't going for a smaller hiking adventure closer to home, instead of travelling to the Northern Territory?'

'Because it's in the heart of this country, so far removed from any mobile service where its guaranteed I'll be completely IT free.' She scanned the obscured landscape and almost whispered into the mist from the heat of her words. 'I need to prove to myself that I'm more than a torso behind a table, and that I'm still me.'

'What does your family say about this?'

Jessica stepped forwards, head down, as he moved in time with her.

'Stop looking down, look ahead.'

'Yes sir,' she said with a giggle.

'They don't know, do they?'

She didn't reply.

'Exactly what has Maggie planned for you with this trip?'

'A six-day hike departing from Alice Springs to do the Larapinta trail.'

'What would your family do if they did find out?'

'They'd try and stop me.'

'Do you have medical clearance?'

'Yes. I showed Maggie the paperwork before she confirmed my bookings. Don't worry, she's made sure there are amenities for me to finish the trek on that week.'

'What's so special about that week to push yourself so much?'

'It was my hell week,' she admitted, looking down to avoid his expression, but still kept moving forwards.

'That's a basic training term.'

'For me, it was waking up after the accident. It'll be my first anniversary in six weeks, and I don't want it to be miserable like last year.'

'Well then…' He leaned over and with his fingertip he lifted her chin. 'Keep your chin up to watch the road ahead and you'll make it.'

She stopped and stared at him as tears threatened to form.

'What did I say wrong now?'

'Um—' She tried to swallow her emotions down. 'No one has said that to me since the accident.'

'If you want it bad enough, you'll do it.'

'Easy for you to say,' she mumbled, 'you're like this pre-dawn guru? Are you smoking some pipe you've been fine tuning to charm more snakes across the road?' Her tinkling laughter echoed as she stepped onto the asphalt. 'Oh wow.'

'What?'

'This is the first time I've made it to the road.' She grinned wider at the vast scene only highlighted by her headlamp where a slight ribbon of light was spotted on the distant horizon.

Inhaling the cool crisp air that was almost sweet against her tongue, she glanced at Brett, who was obviously trying to do the right thing. But he'd also exposed his vulnerabilities to her.

Was he just as scarred as she was, hers worn on the outside, his were hidden on the inside? 'Okay.'

'Okay, what?'

'I'll accept your offer to help me, only if we agree to be brutally honest with each other. No niceties or sugar coating. Say it as it is.'

'You might hate me for it.'

'If it helps me reach my goal, I'll use you.'

'Copping your sass before sunrise there's gotta be better ways to greet the day.'

'I'll be nice, I think? It's rare.'

'I'd believe it.'

'Hey.' She slapped his upper arm that was nothing but solid muscle. 'Stop picking on the walking wounded.'

'You did not just say that?'

'I do have a sense of humour, you know.'

'Lose that with the accident?'

'Yeah, like lots of other things.'

'Like what? Besides your independence?'

'I'm getting that back too.'

'I can see that. Now, gimme this,' he said, snatching one of her poles.

'Hey.' Her balance teetered and she grabbed Brett's jacket, the feel of hard muscles under her palm sent a rush of heat throughout her body.

'Put your hand higher.'

At least he didn't say lower to those tight fitted jeans.

'Rest your hand on my shoulder. I won't bite…much.' He guided her palm higher. 'It'll force you to keep your head up. Don't worry, I won't let you fall. It's how I helped my mate, Mick, train for Kokoda and he has no lower left leg. Come on, let's keep going to the end of my front fence-line.'

'Where's that?' Why was Brett volunteering to train her?

'I'll tell you when.' With a coy grin he strolled beside her. 'I should bring the ute out and follow you like I'm herding cattle. At least I'd have coffee in the cab, heater…'

'You're cruel.' *Cute but cruel.*

'You are aware that the red centre's outback is an unforgiving and cold environment.'

'That's why I dragged myself from a warm bed in winter to do this. What's your excuse?'

'My body-clock is used to being up early, and someone's gotta give you grief,' Brett said.

Jessica had suffered enough grief from her past,

did she really need to add more?

64

# Seven

Saturday morning, Jessica stood inside her cottage geared up for her walk, when a sweep of lights flashed through the kitchen windows as a vehicle pulled up.

'Are you awake yet, Jess?' Called out Brett.

She opened the back door, her hand shielding her eyes from the headlights as Brett jumped out of the driver's side. 'You're not herding me like a cow with your truck, are you?'

'Tempting,' he said with that easy grin, picking up her pack. 'I made coffee and a toasted sandwich for you. Get in.'

'Why?'

'We're going on a road trip. I thought we'd try something different for your training walk this morning.' Brett dumped her pack in the back of his ute, then opened the cab's passenger door. 'See, I'm playing gentleman. Nicole would be so proud.'

She giggled, couldn't help it. But she was curious about his plan, with use of her poles she walked towards him.

'Head up.'

'How? When your headlights are blinding me.' And his whole personality was distracting.

She sipped her coffee while Brett drove through empty dark country roads. 'Now can you tell me where we're going?'

'I've got an engineering gig at this farm in the next town.'

'Sorry, I'm not tool-savvy so I hope you don't expect me to play trade's assistant.'

Brett chuckled as he steered. 'Duly noted, that even in cases of desperate need do not disturb the neighbour to all things engineering.'

'Do you like engineering?' What did Brett do for fun?

'I don't mind it. It's a change from waiting for things to grow and an extra income that keeps the brain active. We're trying to perfect a crop machine we've modified for harvest.'

'Your crops?' She had no idea what grew in the darkened fields they passed.

'No, the Hinton's are trialling soy this season.'

'No gym today?'

'Nope. My weekends are free.'

'You don't like the gym.'

'Not my thing.' He frowned slowing down the ute to take the sweeping bend in the road. 'I'll drop you off on the main stretch.'

'To do what?'

'You'll walk back.'

'Are you kidding me?'

'Don't panic.'

Too late. She wiped clammy hands on her cargo pants, with her heart racing. When he put his hand on her shoulder, the heat from his palm fed a calming warmth that made her breathe easier.

'In the glove box,' he said, leaning over to open it, 'there's a map, a compass, and a GPS. I'm pretty sure we'll have consistent mobile coverage in this area.' He gave her a lesson on using a compass while they drove. 'It's an eighteen-k hike. Flat road. Easy as.'

'Eighteen kilometres?' She gasped as her chest tightened like her ribs were being squeezed in a vice.

'I've estimated you'll be doing that amount each day at Larapinta.'

'Sure. But so soon?'

'The opportunity showed up last night. I didn't have your number, but I knew you'd planned to walk this morning, so why not jump in like you've done so far?'

She couldn't refuse. Even if this was more than she'd bargained for, but was she ready? 'I'll be on my own,' she whimpered without thinking.

'Hey, relax. I'm working just on the other side of that hill. You get stuck you call me and I'll be five minutes away to come and get you. So please, put your number into my phone, then text yourself so you have mine,' Brett said, handing her his mobile. 'You can text me on your progress or if you want me to collect you earlier.'

'You're really serious about this.' Dumping her in the dark. Was she really that cruel to the guy that he was doing this as some cleverly masked payback for her snark?

'Are you serious about doing this six-day hike?'

'Absolutely.' The power of that one word made her sit taller. 'I've been planning to do this since I saw a documentary on the place while I was freezing last winter stuck inside the hospital. And there's no way I'd do the outback in summer.'

'Good.' He pulled the vehicle over, got out of the cab, and jogged around to open her passenger door. 'Look, if you don't finish today, don't stress, you've got time to improve.'

Which made sense, but it didn't lessen the fear in her trembling limbs. 'I have no provisions for you to dump me out here. In the dark. On my own.' There was nothing out here. There were no street lights. No house lights. Nothing.

'Use the torch and you've got poles to whack against the road should any roos say g'day, maybe an odd fox or rabbit. That's about it.'

'Do you swear to that?'

'Do you honestly think I'd leave you out here if you were in any danger?'

She shrugged sheepishly from her safe spot inside the ute. 'Um, no.' That didn't even sound convincing to herself.

'Come on, daylight's coming.' Brett grabbed her hands to pull her gently from the cab, then passed her a thick heavy roll of tape. 'Put this reflective tape around your legs. I'll fix up your pack. I've got you plenty of energy food and water, ten times more than you'll need. Remember, if you're going to the outback, you'll need to sip water regularly to keep hydrated, so best you start getting used to that habit now.'

'Ah huh.' All she could do was nod and listen while she wrapped grey tape around her legs as he shoved assorted items into her backpack.

'Mick and I worked out over the phone on what you'd need per day on your hike. Hope it's not too heavy,' Brett asked, holding out her pack.

'I'm about to find out?' She turned her back to him as he slid the straps over shoulders. It was heavier, but nothing was as heavy as the bricks she'd tried on her first day of training.

'You good?'

She nodded, shifting the load higher on her back. 'Yeah.' She could do this. Maybe?

'All right then, let's strap you in.' Brett talked as he stepped in front of her and adjusted her straps. 'I've put my old rain poncho in this left pocket. It's big enough to cover you and the pack, all you do is fling it over your head like a cape and just keep walking. I've got an old flashing red bike light for the back of your pack for cars to spot you in the morning mists.'

'It's like you're strapping me into a baby's car-seat when you do that.' But he had the knack for finding her spine's sweet spot.

'It needs to be snug. You don't want it rubbing. Also, I've got this small solar light to shine around your legs to use just this once, it'll help you walk in the dark.' He attached it to the bottom of her pack producing a dull light on her boots and the gravel around her.

It brought some comfort to her at the level of thought he'd put into this.

'Now, home is that way.' He pointed down the road, switched on her head lamp and turned her head to face the correct way.

A silent dark road with an even darker skyline stared back at her.

'But—'

'We can have lunch at the bakery when you finish.'

'It's six hours until lunchtime.' She bit her lip, gripping her trekking poles tighter and tried to peer past the reach of his ute's headlights. There was nothing out there.

'You can do this.'

'You've only just met me; how can you say that?'

'Feel free to sit in the car and wait for me if you want? Hey,' Brett said, gently lifting her chin to face the road ahead, 'remember why you're doing this.'

He was right.

'I'm doing this.' Spearing the pole into the dirt on the verge and pushed herself forward.

'Head up.'

'I know.' She snapped back. 'I'm gonna hate you at the halfway point, you know that.'

'Good, it'll make you walk faster.' He then jumped into his ute and said through the open window, 'I didn't think you'd make it to the weekend, so I'm glad you're proving me wrong.'

Her grip tightened on the poles while the pack's

weight straightened her spine. 'You'll have to show me later how you balanced the provisions in this pack and what you put in it.'

'Happy to. Wish I was walking with you,' he said, peering through his front windscreen. 'Keep going straight, watch for the signs and check your map. It's better to get used to both map and GPS. Now, enjoy the scenery.' He drove off, waving.

'Arsehole.'

Yet, she shouldn't complain because she had planned to trek daily—but not like this.

The silence was so loud, and she was so tiny amongst the expansive countryside she couldn't see, and truly felt alone.

Yet, it was like she could hear Brett's voice in her ear, '*remember why you're doing this.*'

This was a test to see how far she could walk.

He'd told her she had time to improve. And she did.

She took a step forward and her boot slid on the gravel in the dark and down she went onto her knees. 'That's just *great.*' Her words echoing in the mist of the cool morning.

She'd fallen on her first freaking step!

Should she hate Brett for this, or hug the man, or both? Which confused her. What did Brett get out of helping her?

She had plenty of time to contemplate an answer with the walk ahead, if she'd managed to start walking.

The gravelly stones dug into her gloved palms as she pushed herself to sit up.

At least no one was around to witness her fall, which is why she purposefully chose to come to Heart Springs to train.

This is what she wanted to do.

Again, like a nag she heard Brett in her ear, telling her, '*so what, you fell over. Now get up and get going.*'

With a groan, she pushed herself up, dusted off her hands and knees, while her pack remained glued to her back. She adjusted her beanie and headlamp. Tucked her scarf over her mouth and nose to ward against the winter air. Gripped her poles and stared down the road ahead.

Eighteen kilometres she had to walk.

That was three kilometres an hour until lunchtime.

The average able-bodied person could do five k's an hour. What was Jessica's average walking speed?

There was only one way to find out.

Jessica took a deep breath and stepped forward. The gravel crunched under boots but it was a small solid step that gave her a decent dollop of courage.

Brett wouldn't have left her out here if he didn't think she could do it.

That thought alone filled her with even more courage to take another solid step forward because very few people, including her parents, believed she could do this. But Brett did.

So now she had to believe in herself.

In just over five weeks, she needed to be prepared for the road ahead. Even if it was alone in the dark.

With everything inside her…she prayed she'd make it.

# Eight

rett sat at one of the outdoor tables set in front of the Heart Springs' bakery to watch the town's main road. Had he done the right thing?

For the hundredth time that day, he checked his mobile. There were no new messages. He was used to that, living a life that included avoiding people.

But not today, when he couldn't stop grinning at Jessica's text messages she'd sent:

*'I saw Bugs Bunny, or was that the Easter Bunny's*

*second cousin? I want chocolate after this…*

*How can I eat your energy snacks when I'm not hungry?*

*All this constant water sipping makes me want to pee — where's your instructions on how to create an outdoor dunny!*

*I hate you but I'm halfway…'*

Her cheeky responses came in every thirty minutes to let him know she was okay.

Sure, Jessica wanted this, but what the hell was he thinking, leaving a female with physical challenges—a beauty—left alone on the side of the road in the dark! It took every ounce of willpower inside him to do that to her.

He'd deserted her when he'd been trained to never leave a man behind.

On the outside, he may have joked around with her. Yet the instant she was out of his line of site he'd worried about her all morning; it'd been driving him insane.

Why had he volunteered to do this?

Life would've been so much simpler, sticking to the farm and not bothering his neighbour for the next five weeks. He could avoid a town full of people easily enough, so why not avoid her too.

He just couldn't put himself through it again, to watch someone, anyone, suffer, only to leave him alone.

It was easier to just stay away.

Then Brett spotted Jessica in the distance. Her head held high, the pack on shoulders and her pole-to-leg stride steady. Very sure and steady.

Pure relief flooded him a mass wave, he palmed his chest as if trying to breathe. He shouldn't be like this, not with a woman he'd just met where they both admitted to irritating each other.

Jessica was challenging herself and he was proud of her efforts.

But she was also challenging him in ways, such as hating himself for leaving a defenceless female roadside.

But then she smiled and waved at him and his heart almost freaking smashed through his rib cage. A fire curled in his lower belly and he licked his lips drinking in the shine of self-pride worn in her eyes.

'I made it.' Jessica smiled wide, stepped up to their table and unclipped the front straps of her backpack.

'Here, let me.' He helped her remove the pack then passed her the drinks he had waiting for her. 'Water and a sports drink for you. Want a coffee?'

'Yes, yes, and yes. And whatever the coach thinks I should eat because I am famished.' Collapsing into the chair, Jessica cracked open the sports bottle and drank deeply.

Brett chuckled at her mostly with relief that her obvious exhaustion hadn't dampened the shine in her smile that reached her eyes. It was gorgeous.

He went inside to order their lunch and soon returned with more water that he placed in front of her. 'Quiche, salad and coffee are coming. Well done on your time today.'

'I don't know if I should hate you or hug you,' she said, pulling out folded pieces of paper from her cargo pants pockets and dumping them onto their table.

'You got my notes?' His lips pursed together waiting for her sassy comeback. He had no idea what possessed him to rip pages from his notebook to scribble out messages, that he'd then taped onto road signs, power poles and fence lines for anyone to read.

'Your breadcrumbs kept telling me not to hate you but to drink, eat, and keep on being merry. I thought I was Alice in Wonderland being led astray by the rascally rabbit in his white ute.'

'I've never done that before,' he admitted sheepishly. 'I thought you'd need reminders to take rest stops. When you said you'd hate me at the halfway mark, why not give you a reason? Did it help?'

'It was great motivation,' she said with a grin. 'Thank you for your notes. Also thank you for getting me there, and for giving me the encouragement to try. It was like I kept hearing you in my ear every time I fell over, to get up and keep moving.'

'You what?' His chest tightened, spotting the dirt on her cargo pants and knees, even on her jacket wrapped around her waist. Dry grass heads and wildflowers were also trapped in straps on her backpack. 'How many times did you fall over?' His voice cracked under the pressure of guilt now twisting his guts.

She waved her hand flippantly at him as she drank.

'How many times?' He would've never let her fall, not near him.

'I'm used to it. Hey, how many people did you tell that I was doing this trek?'

He shrugged, sipping his coffee trying to be as calm as she was. After all, he did find her freshly fallen on the side of their track on her first morning at Kimmel's cottage.

'I had drivers toot their horns and wave at me as they passed. A few slowed down and chatted, while I walked. That was cool. They told me they'd heard I was in trek-training and under your supervision. Did you tell them?'

'It's a small town. I reckon it might've been Nic or Maggie from the travel agency. Not me, I rarely talk to anyone.' He could go for days without speaking to anyone.

'You talk to me.'

'Do we?'

It was Jessica's turn to shrug between sips of water. 'Besides enjoying yourself by torturing me with your notes and trek-training, what do you get out of training me?'

'Honestly?' He didn't have a clue why. He was still trying to process these unknown awakening emotions she was stirring up inside.

'We agreed to be brutally honest with each other where we can openly express at times where I'll tell you I hate you and where you call me irritating—'

'Annoying, confusing, and a strain to my peaceful existence,' he said, mirroring her grin.

'Even though you amped up my fear-factor making me walk alone in the dark, I respect your honesty.'

Did he dare admit it scared the utter crap out of him too, leaving her alone like that.

The waitress arrived with their meals.

'Looks great, I'm starving,' Jessica said, picking up her cutlery. 'I've never eaten so much until I came to this town.'

'Training will do that.'

'And all of this fresh air, and the food tastes better. Is there a farmer's market handy?'

'I can show you after lunch. Can you cook?'

'I come from a household of hit and miss of Mum's many attempts at trying exotic dishes. We still ate it, or attacked Dad's frozen pizza stash.' She took a bite of her quiche and her eyes rolled in obvious delight. 'Yum.'

He couldn't stop watching the way her lips wrapped around her fork as she ate. 'How's it taste?' How would she taste? *Stop it!*

'Divine. This was a great idea for lunch.'

'I haven't been here for years.' He hadn't been anywhere for years. 'I thought it'd be a good spot to wait for you.' Why was he putting himself through all of this worry? People walked roadside daily. Everywhere. So why was she always on his mind?

'Do you hide at your farm?'

'Do you hide in the cottage?'

'I do client visits, but I also enjoy working from home. I don't have to dress up for work or deal with peak-hour traffic racing for carpark spaces like I used to.'

'Did you?'

'What?'

'Dress up?' He held his breath as his chest ached at the vision.

'Pencil skirts and stilettos. Not sure I'll be able to wear heels again, but I gave them to Mum to put away in case. Not that it mattered what I wore because no one saw me in the office.'

'What was your last workplace like?'

'It was either a temperature-controlled room full of computers, that had this constant humming background where it was just me and the machines.'

'Sounds lonely,' said the man who lived alone on a farm.

'Or, I sat in this sea of cubicles where everyone talked on headsets helping people solve their IT issues.

It was noisy, windowless, and right under our supervisors' noses.'

'Now?'

She sat back sipping her water, then smiled looking around the town. 'I have the best view of the winter countryside sitting near a warm fireplace. I even baked a plum cake the other day while waiting on the backup runs, working at my own pace and still achieving my daily goals.'

'Why couldn't you do that before?'

'Not at the office, no way. I started my business at my parents' place, which is in suburbia with a nice-enough garden. They're semi-retired so they're at home hovering. I shouldn't complain, because without their support, who knows where I would've ended up.'

'Back in the government?'

She sighed and the shine dulled in her eyes, picking at her meal with her fork. 'No. To them, I was just another number, easily replaced.'

'Like me in the army.'

'Do you miss it?'

'I miss my mates.'

'You've mentioned Mick.'

'We did basic training together. When Fiona was

sick, they gave me a compassionate discharge while the rest of the crew were shipped to Afghanistan. Where they um…' He faltered. 'I never regretted coming back to be with Fiona, not for a second. I know she would've been there for me if I was in her place.' He'd give anything to trade places so Fiona didn't have to die and leave him so alone. 'Anyway…' Clearing his throat he sipped his coffee. When he looked up, Jessica was staring at him with such a warm and open empathy, he wanted to hold her hand.

Instead, he adjusted his beanie catching her grin at their shared joke. 'Oi, stop picking on my hat habit.'

'Do you keep in touch with your other army mates?'

'They were killed by a road mine.'

'Oh no.' In the blink of an eye she'd grabbed his hand and squeezed it gently.

'It was remote detonated. Bastards were watching for their convoy to pass on their way to help fix up a local school. They were only there to help supply water to that area.' He stared down at her delicate hand that held more courage than he had within himself and gave it a replying squeeze. 'Mick was the only one who survived.'

He faced her with his frown faltering. 'I've, um, never told anyone that.'

'In our own ways, we're both survivors wearing our own battle scars that few people see.'

'What do you do to survive?'

'I keep moving by setting myself some goals.'

'You do like your goals and deadlines.' It was motivating to see her like that.

'My whole life I've always planned it out. But I'm so gonna hate on you tomorrow,' she said with a smile, pulling her hand free to resume eating her meal.

'Because you won't be able to move?'

'I'm sure each step will be painful, but I've been through worse. So, if your ears suffer this burning sensation, or you back tingles like it's being stabbed, it's just me playing voodoo mind tricks.'

'I'd believe it.' Brett grinned, when something shifted within his heart as if an internal wall crumbled into small pieces that fell from his weighted shoulders. 'Breakfast. That's what I want.'

'Excuse me?' She arched an eyebrow at him with her forkful of food halted halfway to her mouth.

'I'm sick of eating my own cooking. So how about, after you've done your morning walk, which is the same time I return from opening the gym, you shout me brekkie?'

'Every day?'

'Except Sunday. Or Saturday.'

'Your toasted sandwich and coffee were nice this morning.'

'Simple stuff I can do, but other stuff no. But if you've got any spare plum cake, I'll play hit and miss taste-tester for you. You should know, I'm also gifted in reading microwave heating instructions and have a great stash of favourites for food-emergencies.'

'How come you don't have other women cooking for you?'

'Nic does when I visit her and Bob, it's been a Sunday tradition for…' He frowned at the table over the habit formed ever since he'd first begun seeing Fiona. 'When my parents retired, I was guaranteed at least one decent meal a week.' And at least one conversation a week. Even if he'd tried to avoid it many times, Nic and Bob wouldn't let him.

She arched her eyebrow at him with a glimmer in her eyes that reflected the world. 'Are you trying to win the pity vote for free meals?'

'It took a lot of planning for this morning's effort.' For a guy who didn't plan much it was huge.

'I gathered that with the snacks you supplied.'

'So, do we have a deal?'

'I don't know who's getting the better part of this agreement...'

He held his breath, surprised he actually wanted this.

'I think we have a deal,' she said, holding out her hand across the table.

He shook her small, soft hand and gave her a sly grin. 'I haven't tried your cooking, yet.'

'You'll be sick of it by the end of five weeks, I bet,' she said, picking up her fork to finish her meal.

'Doubt it. I've got an iron stomach from surviving camp rations.' He quite liked the idea of having breakfast waiting for him in the morning. 'Hey, we should plan next weeks' hike. Have you got that map handy?'

With a mouth full, she nodded and removed it from her pack's side pocket.

He unfolded the map and spread it out between them. 'We'll aim for some uneven terrain next. The National Park's not far with some great trails. I might even come along to annoy you.' That way if she went to fall, he'd make sure he was there to catch her.

He had to remember, Jessica was just another mate who had her own life to lead and leave—then his world would return to normal.

Or would it?

# Nine

'Treat him like my brother,' Jessica said to the empty kitchen as the pan sizzled on the stove and the aroma of sautéed onions filled the air.

How did she get talked into cooking for a man?

She was still sore from this morning's training, even after Brett's stretching tips he'd delivered before he drove away to open the gym. Although he'd left her to walk alone in the dark again, the lane didn't bother her, it was familiar territory now. The difference with this morning was her mind had been so pre-occupied planning what to cook for breakfast, time flew.

Brett was doing so much to help her achieve her goals, she wanted to do right by him. But, if she raised the standard of her meals so high, would he expect that quality daily? Or did she dish up burnt toast so he wouldn't return for seconds?

The guy was growing on her and she was relaxing more seeing him daily. Saturday was brilliant. He'd been so gentle in aiding her in and out of his ute after seizing up over lunch. He even carried her shopping bags at the local farmer's markets, then helped her unpack in her cottage kitchen.

On Sunday afternoon, Brett dropped off a plated roast dinner from Nicole. She was grateful for the free feed and the dozen eggs he'd collected from his place she had yet to see.

But Brett said he liked his privacy, which is why she hadn't dared to peek over the hill and check out his homestead.

Jessica added the tomatoes, mushrooms, and ham off the bone, into the pan making her omelette specialty. Bad luck if Brett didn't like it, then he'd never ask her to cook again.

His ute pulled up, amazed she recognised its sound.

'Door's open.'

'Something smells great,' said Brett, dumping a folded newspaper onto the island bench. 'I brought you the local rag. Thought you might want to check it out as a place to advertise your services.'

'As an escort service—oh wait, that's you escorting me along deserted country roads?' She cocked an eyebrow at him trying not to burst out laughing at his cough.

He ripped off his beanie, shoved it into the back pocket of his jeans, mussing up his hair. 'No. Y'know, your web designing, IT, stuff. What exactly do you do?'

'All sorts. I'm thinking of adding brekkie cook to my list of talents.' She served up the omelette and pushed a plate in front of him on the island bench.

'I'll need to eat it first before you can use me as a reference.' He leaned over and sniffed at the plate. 'Smells safe enough to eat. Are we eating at the bench?'

'The dining table's kinda busy playing office mule.'

Brett checked out her silenced laptops with the extra screens covering the large wooden table where an octopus tangle of electrical cords led to the wall socket. 'That's a lot of electronic equipment.'

'You'd use technology for your engineering creations?' Jessica asked, trying to control the shakes in her hands. She dished out cutlery and napkins, poured the juice and coffee, aiming to have everything within reach before she sat down.

'Not like you. I prefer to design stuff with pencil and paper first.' Brett pulled out the bench stools, scooped up the salt and pepper shakers by the stove, and collected the milk from the fridge on his way back to the bench.

'I enjoy designing graphics, websites, and database creations. I don't do repairs. Although, it seems a few of my clients are trying to steer me more into social media marketing.' No doubt this conversation would bore the guy, as she took a seat beside him, nervously rambling. How did she get talked into this?

'You do all that? From here?' Brett asked, taking a seat on the bench stool and seemed genuinely interested.

'It's easy enough to automate most of it.' She sat stiffly, waiting for Brett to take the first bite.

'I haven't got a clue. I only Skype Mick and do

Facebook for my parents and stuff. You'd do more.' He took a forkful of omelette, chewed, swallowed and prepped for more.

Would he gag and choke any second now? 'It's my job to see what's going on with technology. My dad's all about business and my mum has the creative flair, and it seems I've inherited parts of those traits. You?' Dying to know what he thought of the meal?

Why was she stressing so much over this? It wasn't the first time she'd cooked for someone.

'My move into the army was so we'd cope financially with the drought. It was mum who pushed me to learn another trade in case something went wrong with the farm.'

'You covered your bases?'

'Yep. Bet your Dad told you that if he's into business.'

'One of his many mantras from his preaching playlist.' She giggled, relieved at his smile, with the bonus of him not throwing up from her cooking.

'What are you going to do after you've done Larapinta?'

He looked so serious giving her his full attention it made her heart skip. 'I'm not sure? Which is unusual for me.' She always had a plan with her life carefully mapped out. 'I'll go home to my parents and take it from there.' Her stomach dropped at the prospect of leaving. It seemed like a step backwards if she did. 'I'm only focusing on the hike.' It'd been her biggest goal all year. 'I guess I'll make up my mind while hiking in the outback.'

Brett pursed his lips as his frown faltered, returning his attention to his plate to scrape more omelette onto his fork. 'You've got plenty of work here if you want it. Mrs Gibbens, she breeds show dogs. She asked about you this morning.'

'You talked to other people?' She gasped at him in mock horror, surprised he'd mentioned her. More importantly, what did he say?

'Kind of have to in the gym,' he said, sharing his slow easy side grin that made her morning fretting almost worth it. 'Most customers are trained to not approach me, but Mrs Gibbens is all right. She wants a website for her dogs. She runs obedience show classes, and wants to start a kennel for pampered mutts.'

'I've never done that.'

'Dogs? You ever have pets?'

'Dad does tropical fish. I'm saying, I've never done a site for dog breeders. It sounds like fun. What did you tell her?'

'I showed her your card Nic's got taped on top of the PC. You should give me more of your business cards to leave at the gym. No harm, right?'

'That's a great idea.' Why was Brett going to so much trouble for her? 'Are you sucking-up for me to cook lunch for you too?'

'Maybe,' he said, grinning as he scraped his plate clean. 'There's plenty of work for someone with your skills in this region. If you want it?'

'I'll take it how it comes daily.'

'Good way to be. I don't plan except towards the next harvest.'

'Don't most farmers work on a five-year crop rotation plan? Or do you work on anniversary dates as goal days?'

'Which is what you're doing with Larapinta?'

'I like to know how much I've improved, and to know what I've achieved. Don't you?'

'Nope.' His smile and the shine in his eyes disappeared as he sat back sipping his coffee. 'I try not to look back or see what's ahead.'

'Why not?'

'Then I'm not disappointed when it doesn't happen.' He got up from his seat and took his empty plate to the kitchen sink.

'You and Fiona planned stuff?' She remembered Nicole saying Brett hated change.

'Way back in school, sure.' He turned on the tap and filled the sink with suds as his shoulders slunk and his head lowered. 'But ever since the Army, other people have been doing all the planning for me.'

'Is that why you're planning stuff for me?'

'Am I?' He turned and faced her, raking fingers through his hair where his customary beanie hung out of the back pocket of his butt-beautiful jeans.

'For the week hiking routines and weekend treks you're the one making all the plans. I just agree or—'

'Whine all about it.'

'That, too.' But she wasn't going to whine about the guy doing her dishes. *Nice.*

Gripping the bench top, she pushed off her chair, walked around the bench with her hand skimming the counter top to return the juice and milk to the fridge.

'I have the advantage of knowing this area. I'm

glad to see you're not using the crutches when you're inside.' He pointed to her trekking poles and metal crutches resting alongside her boots by the back door.

'I've got walls and stuff.'

'But there's gaps where you walk unaided.'

'I'm improving daily. And you didn't answer my question, is that why you plan for me? As the complete stranger, I'm not saying I hate it, I'll admit I needed a plan and a personal trainer for this.'

'I'm no bloody gym bunny.'

'No way, Mr Farmer,' she said, waving her hand over his dirt-stained jeans that hugged him in all the right places. He'd be sexy if he just wore a woman's apron while washing dishes.

Brett sighed with a frown as he carried her dish to the sink. 'I guess I am planning stuff for you.'

'For the free feed?' Relieved, he mirrored her grin as he washed her plate.

'It's easy, you're a clean cook. Fewer dishes. Thanks for a top feed.' He grinned, patting his flat stomach hidden by his woollen work shirt that stretched over his biceps and chest. 'Well, best I get on with it and for you to play on that keyboard. Thanks for brekkie.' He winked at her, opened the door, and slid on his beanie heading into the sunlight. 'See ya in the morning, same time.' And was gone, as if a vacuum had sucked his presence leaving only his masculine outdoorsy aroma to linger behind.

She hugged herself watching his ute drive away and only then did she sigh with relief. He liked her cooking.

But why try so hard to make him happy when they were just friends? New friends, because it'd only been a week.

Was Brett still grieving for his wife?

Understandable if they'd been together since school. How long had he been widowed? She has so many questions she wanted to ask him—did she need to know the answers?

Jessica rarely revealed anything personal with anyone. Yet, the confessions flowed easily with the conversations she shared with Brett. She'd never been so openly honest with anyone, except with Brett.

And he was only here for the convenience of her cooking breakfast as a drive-thru, and she was improving in her walking working with him. Besides, no man would come near her for anything other than friendship or work, which is what this was—a business deal, for the next month, nothing more. Simple.

Yet she couldn't help but think of what she'd cook for him tomorrow. *Ugh,* who was she?

# Ten

Jessica grunted as she tipped over the large tractor tyre in the paddock, then stood hunched over with palms resting on her thighs, catching her breath. 'Do you do this at the gym?'

'No. I'd have Bob on my back for staining his floor,' replied Brett, leaning on her hiking poles, supervising.

'You don't like the gym, do you?'

'I know you don't.'

'I'll admit it's true.'

'Because of your leg?'

'I never enjoyed the whole gym experience. My thing is sweating in silence outside because I sit inside all day. This makes a nice change,' she said, waving to the wide-open paddock. 'But not lately, with you watching over my shoulder.' She elbowed him in the ribs; pleased for his laugh.

'You agreed, or volunteered.'

'I'm grateful for all your help. Thank you.' Brett had been there supplying daily drive-by training tips on his way to the gym, then they'd share breakfast and talk with ease. When Brett didn't open the gym, he'd stroll beside her and they'd listen to the morning sounds of the expansive countryside.

In the six weeks together, he'd become a friend. A good friend.

'Even though I hated you at times, I've improved heaps under your regime. I'm becoming more like you.'

'Yeah, how?' Brett shared his slow easy side-grin that made her catch her breath.

Forced to turn away to focus, she squatted to grip on the black rubber of the dirty tyre. Dirt scraped under her nails as she lifted, groaned, moaned, and grumbled under its weight.

'Use your legs. Trust them.'

Her boots dug into turf and her legs trembled as she strained. 'Yes, Yoda. Or is that Obi-Wan,' she muttered as she fought gravity with the tyre teetering on its rim.

'The force of cheekiness is strong with this one,' he mimicked.

'Not right now, it isn't.' She shouldered the rubber, and it keeled over to bounce on the ground and then settled. There she plonked down onto its top edge in the middle of the paddock and admired the lush landscape.

'Here,' Brett said, passing her the water bottle.

'Thanks.' She took a long drink as he sat beside her on the tyre.

'How do you feel?'

'My arms are burning and so is my bum.'

'Glutes.'

'Whatever. You do this field torture well.'

'Yeah, I'm kinda having some basic training flashbacks here.'

'You don't strike me as the gung-ho Army type.'

'I didn't mind it. I joined to set up my nest egg, and stay long enough to receive the Army pension and then play here. This farm has been in the family for generations, and I've always planned to stay here and buy my parents out so they could retire.' He loved the farm; the way his eyes shone at the scenery and the pride she heard in his voice every time he spoke about the place.

'You actually had a plan?'

'Says the person who doesn't when she finishes her hike.'

Which was true, she still had no idea where to go, except back to her parents' place. Which was so unlike her, she always had plans to meet her end goals.

'I remember you telling me you enlisted to keep this place going through the drought.' She couldn't picture this place dry and barren, when it was now thriving. 'Why do you work at the gym if you don't like it?'

Brett frowned as he pulled at a tuft of grass. 'Fiona wanted it.'

'Were you married before you joined the Army?'

'I can't remember a time when we weren't together. Most of my childhood memories have Fiona in them.'

'Did Fiona transfer with you?'

'For a few years. Then she got homesick and came back.'

'To the farm?' Jessica gazed at the homestead nestled among fertile farmlands, it was so beautiful and peaceful out here. She couldn't stop staring at it.

'Fiona never stayed here. She hated shifting when I'd get transferred to a new base. When she heard the YMCA lost its funding, Fiona recruited her parents and me to help her buy the business to create her gym. She loved it.'

'You didn't?'

'Nope. Being a personal trainer was Fiona's thing, where she'd run the classes and I'd maintain the machinery. Being semi-retired, her dad, Bob, was content to push a broom at night, while Nicole did the admin. It worked well when I wasn't here, too.'

'How long were you married?'

'Two weeks.'

'I'd assumed you'd married sooner?'

'We'd planned to marry when I finished with the Army and move in here. But I kept extending my time, making good money. I was enjoying my overseas tours knowing I was making a difference. Fiona wanted to stay at the house near the gym. My parents were happy to keep living here on the farm. So, it kept getting pushed back until she was diagnosed at the hospital and all our plans changed.'

'Hospitals have this knack of changing people's priorities.' She sighed, refusing to remember her time in hospital. 'Where you did get married?'

'In the hospital's gardens just before Fiona died. We didn't even have time to choose wedding rings. Our parents and some of the hospital staff were witnesses… We always planned to marry. Grow old together. Pass this farm on to our kids. Now…'

'I'm so sorry.' She gave his shoulder a tender squeeze, feeling the burden of grief he seemed to still be carrying.

'Not your fault,' he said, giving her hand a pat. 'I'm a complacent prick who should've married her sooner. Not when it was too late to enjoy it. I kept thinking we had all the time to do it later. And then we didn't have enough time…'

She stared at the skyline dotted with white clouds while they sat quietly, the breeze carried the rich earthy aroma.

'Why aren't you married or got someone?' Brett

asked.

Jessica shrugged, picking at her bootlaces. 'I thought I did.'

'Don't tell me you pushed him away like you've done with everyone else trying to help you.'

'Hey, I'm getting better.'

'You are,' he said, mirroring her grin.

'I wasn't always like that. I had a boyfriend…and, um, when I was all messed up, he couldn't cope.'

'This guy didn't dump you, did he?'

'We agreed to split so I could concentrate on recovering.'

'Tell me he did not walk away?'

'You could see how relieved he was when I'd told him it wasn't a good time.'

'How'd you take that?'

'He didn't love me as much as I'd hoped. It was then I accepted I'd always be alone. My brother still avoids me, because it's how he copes. I don't blame him; I know I've changed.' She could never blame them.

'Everyone changes and people cope differently.'

'But you never left Fiona, that is so rare. Sure, I had my parents, and work sent flowers but no one else missed me.'

'Surely someone must have missed you?'

'My fault. I was such a geek, so focused on my career. In the end, I was nothing more than just a voice on the phone, fixing IT issues, stuck in a windowless office, staring at a screen. Except for my boss, he freaked out.'

'Good.'

'Not really. He was freaked out over the worker's compensation paperwork. That's when I realised, I was just another number and decided to work for myself. I haven't regretted it since.' She hugged her bent legs and said, 'I love my job and how it changes, forcing myself to meet new people. With the insurance payout, my savings, and my credentials, I knew I'd be okay. Besides, I could always suffer in silence at my parents' place if I went broke.'

'Come on,' he said, nudging her playfully, 'you must have some idea about what you're going to do after Larapinta?'

'I keep drawing a blank.' She shrugged, still not sure on what to do after the hike. 'My focus has been on getting to Alice Springs and completing the Larapinta trail. I came here to train and prove to myself I'm still me.

I just didn't expect to get the amount of work when I arrived.' Or to find a friend in Brett.

'You're charging me a freaking fortune on the gym's website, you know that.'

'If you hadn't been such a prick, I'd might've given you a discount,' she said, poking his arm.

'Oi, I've been nice to you. I never complained about your cooking, once.'

'You wouldn't want to! Although, making me roll dirty tractor tyres in mud all over your paddock isn't nice.' She was covered in dirt.

'You wanted to go hike in the desert, not me.'

'Thank you, Brett, because of your help I know I can do it.' She leaned over and kissed his cheek. But he turned and their lips were just a breath apart. 'I'd, um…'Clearing her throat, she pushed herself up and smiled wide. 'Did you see that? I didn't need the sticks to stand.'

'Well done. Do you think you can walk across the paddock without them?'

'I'm too sore, which isn't going to look pretty hobbling for a few days. Can't believe I'm having a farewell dinner tomorrow.' She was touched Maggie and

Nicole had organised with a few others to meet at the pub.

'I'll pick you up at six.' Brett held out her sticks, gripping onto them she was back in her comfort zone. With a fingertip, he brushed her stray hair out of her eyes tucking it behind her ear. 'You always looked beautiful. Even with dirt on your face.' He brushed his thumb against her cheek, then gazed at her for a moment as his thumb slid slowly across her bottom lip.

He was so close.

Breath held, her gaze locked with his and everything around them paused as he drew her closer with his palm cradling her cheek.

'Don't.' She stepped away from him, even though she wanted to melt into his chest—she couldn't. 'We're friends, okay. I'm sorry if I gave you the wrong impression. I can't.' She stabbed the hiking poles into the earth with more force than needed as she turned away from him. 'You deserve better than me. We both know I'm leaving; it's how it was always planned. I'm sorry.' Brett deserved nothing but the best. Someone better than her.

How come no other woman in town had snatched him up? Brett was gorgeous, funny, smart, gentle, almost perfect. She had daydreamed of being with him. Her body ached near him, and she missed him when she didn't see him.

But in her dreams of shared passion, she was always whole.

She'd never be good enough for Brett, or for any man, and accepted that.

He was only kissing her out of pity, loneliness, and the convenience of her being here too. Nothing more.

Brett wasn't ready for anyone else, still grieving for his wife. And he certainly didn't need the extra burden of caring for someone like her.

She'd come out here purely to train for her trip to Alice Springs and needed to focus on the destination ahead, because in two more sleeps she'd be standing in the heart of Australia.

# Eleven

Her hair wouldn't sit straight, her makeup was wrong, and she'd tried on everything in her suitcase—twice. It was just dinner with friends for her last night in Heart Springs.

*Why am I so nervous?*

Because it felt every bit like a date.

Giving up, she let her hair tumble free past her shoulders. Slipped on her flat shoes and checked her reflection in the mirror. Her blue woollen dress hugged her body, toned from all the work Brett made her do. It was the fittest she'd ever been.

She heard Brett's ute pull up, soon followed by a knock and the creak of the back door opening. 'Oi, you ready?'

'Yes.' *No.*

'Wow.' Brett stood still as his jaw dropped.

'It's all wrong, right?' She tugged at the hem of her dress, praying it wouldn't catch on her leg brace.

'No. Come on.' He wrapped her hand around his arm, then grabbed her coat and bag.

'My crutches.'

'Not tonight.' Pocketing the house key, he shut the door behind them.

'But—'

'Relax,' he said, opening the ute's door. 'It's just dinner with the crew as your bon voyage.'

'This feels like a date,' she blurted out as she climbed into the passenger seat.

'I've never really dated so I wouldn't know.'

'But what about you and Fiona, you must've had date night or something?'

'I'd known Fiona as a kid where our idea of dating

was sharing lunch in the school yard. Besides, if this *was* a date, you wouldn't go because *you* don't date. Now relax, you look beautiful. You always do.' He closed her door and ran around to take the driver's seat.

Jessica blushed and cracked the window open for the cool air. Brett was just being polite. *We're friends, nothing more.* 'I could've driven and then you'd be free to drink.'

'You'll be doing enough driving tomorrow to the city, let me do this. Have a few drinks, you deserve it.'

'But, I've—'

'Stop.' He grabbed her hand and made her face him. 'You've worked your butt off to achieve your goals, so be proud of yourself, okay.'

'I should tape your little ego-boosting speeches to play while I'm hiking. I'm definitely packing your best roadside rogue-notes you've written for me.'

On her solo morning trails, she'd discover his notes of roadside inspiration reminding to eat, drink, rest, or stretch. It was simple pieces of papers he'd tape on road signs, power poles, trees, or fence lines. Yet, to see one of them flapping in the distance when she was exhausted, only made her walk faster.

She'd kept them all.

'Mmm, there's a thought.' He grinned at her as he started the ute and headed for their shared lane.

'You're not going to record yourself—'

'And send them in a phone message, good idea,' he said as he steered them closer to town.

'I was only kidding.' But the way his eyes twinkled in the dying sunlight and that slow easy grin showed he'd do it too.

Brett had helped her achieve more than she'd thought possible. 'How can I thank you for all you've done for me?

'You cooked. And you're shouting dinner tonight.'

'Yeah, but…'

'Just enjoy it.' He pulled up at the Heart Springs Hotel. Before she'd unclipped her seatbelt, Brett was there, opening her door.

'I've always wanted to see the view from the pub's balcony.' Gripping his muscular arm for balance, she had to admire his aroma of soap and freshly shampooed hair. He was still far too sexy for a friend.

'Do you want to try those steps before dinner?'

'Didn't we agree I'd reserve my strength for the hike.'

'This isn't hiking, it's a set of stairs. Come on.'

Brett always encouraged her to step beyond her comfort zone. 'Well, it is my last night in town, why not?'

'That's my girl.' He grinned, giving her a wink.

*His girl?* No, she wasn't. Yet hearing him say it made her heart bloom. If she could skip, she would. Besides, Brett was all about assisting mates with their achievements.

'I'll be right behind you.'

She was fearless with Brett being there. But he wouldn't be there forever, and her heart squeezed at the thought.

Jessica grabbed the bannister's cool wood and gazed upwards. 'I miss my pole.'

'I'm here if you need me. You can do it.'

'You say that a lot,' she said, taking the first step.

'Look up, not at the stairs. And what do I do?'

'Push me.' The gentle touch of his palm on her lower back gave her all the encouragement in the world.

'Is that a bad thing?'

She stepped again, and again, and onto the landing with a huge smile on her face. 'Today, it's a good thing.' She stood tall, and fisted the air with pride. '*I did it.*'

Brett shared his easy side-grin. 'You sure did.

C'mon, view's this way.' He led her out to the balcony where the winter breeze was invigorating and she gazed over Heart Springs' main street.

She smiled at the oversized steps that stood out front of the travel shop, now with a new handrail. This was bigger than that. It was another personal hurdle she'd overcome, ever since she'd come to this town. Even with its closed shops the place had become familiar to her where she knew the owners by name, not just as clients, but friends.

Something tugged inside her heart. 'I'll miss this town, and its people.'

'We'll miss you, too.' Still holding her hand, Brett's thumb brushed her skin sending a shiver to spread up her arm. 'I'll miss you.'

Admiring the fine lashes that outlined his eyes, did she dare believe him?

'I know you can't see past the walk and I get that. But you can come back.'

'I'd never planned to.' Everything in her life had always been planned, and meticulously mapped out, right up to this moment. But there was nothing past the six-day hike in the Northern Territory. She didn't know if to be scared or exhilarated by it, not knowing what came next. Only focusing on completing this trek.

Brett frowned slightly at the town spread out below them. 'After Fiona died and I left the Army, everyone did all the planning for me. Except you. You let me plan your training and weekend hiking trips, which makes me want to plan my future and not have others do it for me.'

'Are you ready to move on?'

'It's been three years since Fiona died, and I'm still hanging onto something that doesn't make me happy. While you're here doing something amazing for the first anniversary of your accident. You've moved on by turning a negative into a positive. I want to do that too.' Brett inhaled deep and announced, 'I'm selling my share of the gym to Kelly.'

'B-b-but, what about the mornings you open. Don't you use that to socialise?' *To not be a hermit.* It worried her he'd return to that way of life again once she'd gone.

'I got used to you being here, giving me grief in the mornings. I don't like change —'

'I heard.'

'But I like how much you changed my world the minute you entered it, and I want you to come back.' His warm palm cupped the side of her face.

'I can't.'

'Why not?'

'I'm—'

'There you are,' said Nicole coming from the staircase.

'Brett got me to do the stairs,' said Jessica, relieved Nicole had stopped an awkward conversation.

'Well done, Jessica, and you look so lovely tonight. Brett, good to see you got rid of that beanie. Now let's get you back down the stairs, we're all waiting.' Nicole hooked her arm around Jessica's and with Brett on the other side, they escorted Jessica to her farewell dinner and her last night in Heart Springs.

# Twelve

'I'm scared,' Jessica said as the sun shone through the kitchen windows. Brett sat opposite her at the dining table, now vacant of her computers, sharing their last breakfast together that had been Brett's payment for trek-training.

Except this morning, Brett cooked breakfast while she packed. He'd carried her bags to the car while she tidied up the cottage to look like she'd never even been here. Yet, this tiny place surrounded by the large land, held many fond memories for her.

'Do you want me to come with you to make sure you get on that plane?' Brett asked.

Jessica wanted to say yes. But this was hard enough without prolonging the pain she was shouldering by leaving him.

She was never supposed to care for the guy in a way that went much deeper than being his friend.

Brett didn't need to carry the burden of caring for her either.

'I'm leaving my car at my parents' and I'm forcing my brother to take me to the airport. He owes me.'

'The brother who won't talk to you?'

'Yeah, I'm going to use the drive-time to sort out our issues.'

'Good for you. Have you told your parents what you're doing?'

'Oh yeah,' she said, grinning behind her coffee cup.

'Are they trying to talk you out of going?'

'Of course they are. I only told them so it'd help force me onto that plane.'

'Why?'

'Whenever they say I can't do it, I'll prove to them I can.'

'You clever little rebel.' He chuckled over his coffee, then glanced around the empty room. 'You know, Maggie hasn't rented this place out yet. You can come back.'

'I'm not making any commitment to anything except this trip.' She sighed so deep it dragged her shoulders down as she stared at the grains on the worn wooden tabletop. 'Am I kidding myself?' Was her question about her hike in central Australia or how much she cared about Brett?

His hand covered hers as he said, 'You'll do great.'

'I don't want to inconvenience the tour guides.'

'Maggie's already sorted the tour guides out and I've told them not to treat you like a princess, just a stubborn mule who is quite capable.'

'You did not.'

'I wanted to make sure you were prepared and they gave me tips to train you.' Brett reached out and pulled her to her feet. He then escorted her to the car, carrying her sticks in hand as he aided her to walk like they'd done many times. 'You will do this. I believe in you to do this.'

'Why?'

'Because I'm hoping once you see how magnificent

you are, you'll let others in, too.'

'Like who?'

'Me.'

She barely gasped, yet it was as if the countryside held its breath with her as he leaned closer and with the feather touch of his lips against hers it curved her entire universe. Melting into his chest as his arms embraced her, his lips captured hers. The sensation filled her heart with warm happiness that spread to her fingers and toes, silencing all her second-thoughts. Under the power of his kiss it was like tasting her dreams.

But this wasn't a dream.

This kiss was real.

Brett couldn't resist any longer, something shattered inside him making him deepen the kiss, pulling her chest to chest. The blood roared in his ears at the sweep of her tongue against his, it almost sent him into a spin.

She tasted better than he'd ever imagined.

His hands tumbled through her soft locks, wanting to devour her. Yet, before it got any more heated, he pulled back and gazed into her caramel-coffee eyes. His thumb traced her beautiful plump lips, memorising every intricate detail. He didn't want to, but he had to let her go.

She needed to do this for herself, and he helped her take her seat behind the steering wheel.

It was up to Jessica now.

'Drive safe,' he said with a husky voice, so close to begging her to stay. But she wouldn't and they both knew it. 'Text me when you get to the airport and when you arrive in Alice Springs.' But would she? Was this the end of all their communications?

'I will.'

'Be safe, please, and remember to look at that bigger picture.' He hoped she would. Which only made him think harder about his own future too. 'And don't you dare take that laptop.'

'I won't.'

'Enjoy it. Okay.'

'I'll try.'

'You will.' Holding her door open, he leaned down and brushed her lips with his. 'Go, or you'll miss your flight.' It reminded him of all those times he left the Army with his eyes only on the adventure ahead and not at what he'd left behind.

This time he was the one who was staying, and it gutted him to be on this side. He did not want to be left behind.

Yet he had no choice.

Jessica wasn't going to stay, and if she did, she'd eventually come to hate him and then she'd blame him for missing this big personal goal of hers.

This week was Jessica's, and all he could do was let her go… for good.

'Thank you, for everything.' The tears welled in her eyes, and her heart seemed so heavy in her chest it ached. Her lips tingled, his taste lingered, and her body was cold away from his embrace. How could she feel all that that from one kiss?

'You can thank me by sending me a selfie on top of that mountain on your anniversary date.'

'I will.' *Hell yeah.*

Brett closed her door and stepped back. His

delicious denim eyes and the chiselled cheekbones that shadowed his features reminded her of a charcoal sketch destined for a museum wall. With the sunrise spreading across lush farmlands behind him, it was just the way she wanted to remember him. Even wearing his black beanie, Brett was glorious.

Jessica's smile faltered. Her excitement for her future dimmed. Giving a limp-wristed wave, she watched him from her rear-view mirror as she drove away from the cottage that had been home for six weeks.

But it felt more than that.

This town and its people had been so good to her, making her feel a part of the community in her short time here. Many had slowed down to chat with her while driving alongside as she trekked the many country roads. Everyone who passed, always gave her a friendly wave. There were the clients she'd met, and the other people she'd been introduced to while exploring the place alongside Brett. All were welcoming. There may be a life in Heart Springs, if she wanted it.

But she needed to do this trek first.

If she stopped now, she'd always wonder if she could, and if she stalled, she'd never go.

But would she return?

She had no reason to.

Yet leaving Brett behind hurt more than anything she'd ever physically been through before.

# Thirteen

Checklists checked and rechecked. Boots polished and laced. Her day-pack loaded and snuggly strapped into that sweet spot on her spine. With poles in her gloved hands, Jessica faced the start of the red dirt trail. The desert wind nipped at her skin and the sunrise started in the biggest cloudless sky she'd ever seen. It was like staring at an upside-down sea that stretched into infinity.

The suntanned guides with their wide-brimmed Akubras, checked over each hiker's pack, straps, boots, while their leader talked about the day's trek ahead. He introduced his team then everyone had to introduce themselves.

The first to speak was a couple, holding hands like newlyweds. 'Hi, we're from Manchester,' he said in a thick Mancunian accent. 'We're 'ere on a travel visa for a year. And we've got a bit of a confession to make, haven't we, luv.' He looked to his lady who gave a sheepish shrug, as he continued. 'You see, we're a bit hung-over and tired from this long bus-ride to get 'ere from Darwin.'

'Yeah, well, that'll do it, eh,' said the tour leader with a wry grin on his deeply tanned complexion. 'You're not the first, and ya won't be the last to say that about the trip to Alice.' The other tour guides nodded as he removed a small cylinder from his pocket and popped the lid with his thumb in one well-practised move. 'Take a coupla of these with water before we go, eh. It'll help.'

'Cheers, mate. We're really sorry,' the pair mumbled in their thick accents while taking the medication.

Jessica grinned at the partners-in-crime who chuckled to themselves like naughty school kids. They looked like fun to be with.

The next to speak was a couple enjoying their thirtieth wedding anniversary. They made Jessica swoon with warmth at the obvious adoration shared between them.

The wife, holding her husband's hand, addressed the group. 'Besides walking daily, we plan a hiking adventure, once a year. It's a reminder of our first date that was awful,' she said to the small group, snickering while her husband's smile widened. 'We went on a hike-date and got lost, and got bitten by every known insect out there. Our faces and arms got scratched by every low-lying branch, I thought they were attacking us on purpose. But, when we finally got to the road, the *next day*—' The group gasped.

'I kissed that tarmac,' said the husband, raising his hand in the air. 'Then I asked her to marry me while still kneeling on that road in the middle of a national park.'

'Did you say yes?' asked the female backpacker.

'Luv, they're married thirty years,' said her partner, with his arm around her shoulders giving her a slight squeeze.

The family of four, from Adelaide, wore matching red ski-jackets and wide smiles. This time it was their teenage daughter, with headphones dangling around her neck, who spoke. 'Um, yeah, well, we're here coz Dad's mad keen for it. He's been dragging me and my baby brother out for years. He calls it our Wi-Fi free family time.'

'I'm a writer,' said the father, 'I sit in front of my laptop at home—'

'With constant uninterrupted Wi-Fi,' complained the teenage son, frowning at his mobile in hand.

'Do you go through Wi-Fi withdrawals?' Jessica asked the young guy.

'Oh yeah, all the time.' Shaking his head, he slid into his top pocket, zipped it shut, then looked at the expansive scenery surrounding them. 'But...as Mum always says, it'll be there when we get back.'

'Huh?' Jessica bit her bottom lip as she stared at her silent mobile in hand. There were no bars. No signal. Nothing.

She held it up in the air trying to find a signal, something.

But there was nothing.

Her expensive, updated smartphone was now reduced to an old-fashioned electronic, personal organiser, similar to the one she'd bought with her brother for their dad on Father's Day when they were teenagers. The only difference was this one had a camera.

'You look like you're about to suffer Wi-Fi withdrawals there, Miss?' said the father of the small family group.

Jessica cringed and looked up from her phone's screen to find everyone watching her. 'Um, yeah, I think so.' She confessed, lifting her shoulders. 'I'm an IT consultant. I do web designs and I'm always on the Wi-Fi,' she said, holding up her practically dead phone. 'Except for airports, I've never been out of range like this.'

'Yeah well, you're gonna be completely out of range from the rest of the world for the next six days, eh,' said the tour leader.

Jessica tried to swallow the lump in her tight throat. 'It's why I'm here.' She slid her phone into her top pocket, not quite ready to close it up completely, just yet.

She should've listened to her dad and hired a satellite phone for the week. For what? To check her emails?

No, she chose this place for a reason and that was to be IT-free. Completely.

She just didn't think it'd be this bad.

The rest of the group introduced themselves. There was a photographer and his videographer mate, a few eager bird watchers and some long-term hikers. They'd come from around the world to be here.

And then they were off.

The head guide walked and talked at the front of the group. There was a guide in the middle, and another trailed in the back with the small group in between them.

One step after the other, Jessica followed their lead. Her grin grew and she had a sudden bout of the giggles from the adrenalin rush of excitement that washed through her.

She was actually here.

She was finally doing this—but something was missing. What had she left behind?

Pink bottlebrushes dripped with honeyed dew filling the air with their fragrance. She stepped through the low grasses that grew in clumps between red dust and shoal.

It was a place of pure fresh air. Of no cars. No phone towers. No buildings. Just space and the story of its people.

The untouched beauty beckoned her as she took a

photo of the setting, but knew it'd never do justice to the magnificence before her. But she had promised Brett she'd take the photo at the start of her journey.

Her heart squeezed. *I miss him.*

Sliding her phone back into her pocket, she patted the folded pieces of paper she kept close to her heart. They were all of Brett's roadside notes of inspiration, and she was suddenly wishing he was here to do this with her. But that was impossible.

She was here now, so she gripped her poles and took that first step into the wilderness.

# Fourteen

Grief was like a toxic old friend that Brett knew well.

It was like someone had lopped off the top of a bottle of stout with a machete, allowing the jagged edges to release all the frothy goodness of life to flow freely. The bottom of the bottle would have just enough left to attract nosy flies that would drown in the sticky sediment like an empty corpse to toss into the rubbish.

Grief was also the one cup, one plate, one knife, one fork, and the one spoon that rested on his kitchen sink.

Grief was also the sound of silence.

The howl of the cold wind pushed against his open back screen door as the grey rain pelted against his house. Fine mists brushed against his cheeks as he leaned back in his kitchen chair, rested his head against the wall and watched the outside world. It was as grey and dull as he was.

It was never meant to be like this.

He glanced at his silent phone laying on the table.

Before he'd met her, Brett rarely turned on his mobile. Now, it was always within arm's reach.

Why was he bothering? She was truly out of range now. It sucked.

There were no photos of the sunrise from her morning walks. No random meme's or one-line jokes found during her days online. No text messages to tell him breakfast was ready or requests to collect milk on his way back from opening the gym. Now, there were no cooked breakfasts waiting for him. And no more daily conversations.

It was never meant to be like this.

It was never permanent.

She was only visiting for six weeks, with that first week trying to avoid each other because they'd argue.

Both admitting they were irritated by the other.

He'd never been like this with Fiona. He knew everything about Fiona from way back when they were learning how to read side by side in school. It was that bond of knowing someone so well all your life.

But this was different. Getting to know someone who'd infiltrated his life in so many ways that he couldn't bring himself to drive down his own lane. It hurt to see the cottage, so cold and empty. Once it used to bring him joy seeing the lights glow from the kitchen windows, and that chimney flowing with warmth.

Jessica had done it here in his own kitchen. Her perfume would mix with the warm cooking aromas as they cooked side by side, experimenting on some new dish Jessica's mum had recommended. The stereo would play in the background, and her crutches were left by the back door. Half-drunk glasses of wine would rest on the table among the assorted maps from teaching her how to chart courses for their weekend hikes. He'd shown her his images of the Kokoda trek, admitting to the struggles he'd gone through. Along with many things he'd never shared with another living soul.

Now he was left with nothing but an empty table

and only one cup, one plate, one knife, one fork, and one spoon resting on his kitchen sink.

He should have never gone near her. He should have never listened to Nicole who'd made him help Jessica. He was only supposed to apologise, offer recommendations to help and then leave her to it.

But no, he thought it'd be okay to help her more, knowing she was only here for such a short time.

He should be used to this emptiness, now she'd left him.

Unlike Fiona's passing, he'd wanted her to find peace. Brett had prayed for her to be free from the pain she was suffering from the sickening curse of cancer.

He missed them both. One he'd known all his life. The other, less than two months. They were also the opposite of each other. Would the two have been friends if they'd ever met?

But that old feeling of grief was back again.

It shouldn't be, not in this house. It's why he hid here. With Fiona passing, everything in town reminded him of her. He'd kept expecting her to walk around the corner. Instead, he copped the sorrowful looks from the townspeople giving their condolences on his loss. Sure, they missed her too, but he missed her more.

But this place, his childhood home, had been his place of solace. He had many fond memories of growing up here and it had always been his dream of making it his home. He'd renovated the kitchen, the bathroom, and had many other projects planned to make it the home it always was.

Now it was an empty cold shell.

As cold as the cottage along the front lane.

A sweep of lights caught his attention through the pouring rain as a car came up his long drive.

'Damn.' It was Nicole. He sat up, scrubbing at the bristles on his face and looked around. The place was clean. Cold. But clean.

Brett pushed up from his chair, all stiff and sore, wearing the same clothes for days. Probably the last time he'd showered and shaved too. He opened the backscreen door, to meet Nicole rushing up to the veranda.

'Hope you've got the kettle on, Brett,' said Nicole as she reached up and kissed his cheek. 'You look terrible.'

'I'm fine.'

'Ah, huh?' She put the covered plate on the table

and peered around the kitchen. 'You missed the roast.'

'Wasn't hungry,' he mumbled, putting on the kettle, sliding back into his chair to watch the outside world through his kitchen door.

'It's freezing in here.' Nic slammed the backdoor shut and started tinkering around in his kitchen.

He didn't mind the cold, it helped him stay numb.

'Have you heard from her?' Nicole asked.

'Who?'

'You know who. Jessica?'

'She's out of range.' *Gone, like everybody else.*

'Reminds me of what it was like when you'd be out of range for work in the Army. It used to drive your parents and Fiona nuts, where she'd be at the gym working out all the time.'

Brett never understood that feeling. Until now.

Dragging the small heater in with her, Nicole closed the connecting hallway door. The boiling kettle rattled on the bench while she talked.

Brett adored the woman, who was a second mother, but he didn't hear a single word she said.

Nicole plonked a steaming cup of tea in front of him and took a seat at the table. 'So, you're selling the gym to Kelly.'

'The lawyer said it'd be another few weeks for the paperwork.'

'What are you going to do with your spare time?'

He shrugged. 'I needed to let go, Nic.' He was done hanging on to a job he didn't like.

'I get it. You're ready to move on, but this…' She waved her hand over at his scruffy attire.

'I'm saving water.' Which was lame, when it was pouring and his rainwater tanks and dams were almost full, with the weather predicted to continue.

He stared back at the rain that streaked his windows like tears. He wanted to open that door again.

Nah, he should've let that door stay shut. Like he should've never gone near Jessica and kept his distance as the neighbour no one saw.

He was sick of people coming into his life and leaving.

It wasn't Jessica's fault. She told him right from the start she was only here for six weeks.

But a lot had happened in that time. He'd found a friend and then lost her.

'Here,' said Nicole, dropping a glossy brochure onto the table. He recognised it from Maggie's store.

'What's that?'

'An itinerary.'

'For where?'

'Larapinta.'

His sighed and his chest sunk lower. He should be happy for Jessica and truly wanted her to succeed this week. 'I know her itinerary.' They'd spent hours going over it, side by side, checking out the landscape on her many screens in her office area of the cottage.

'Open it.'

'Why?'

'Just open it, young man.'

He rolled his eyes, snatching up the card he flicked open the itinerary. He read the words Northern Territory, Alice Springs, with a brief explanation of the 223-kilometre walking trail that ran along the West MacDonnell Ranges.

Jessica was only trekking half of the Larapinta trail which included Mount Sonder, and it was that mountain climb that Jessica was worried about the most.

A gust of wind rattled the screen door as the rain pelted harder against the house. Not like it would be in the Northern Territory where winter in the red-centre was rain-free, it was their Dry season, the perfect weather for hiking.

God, he missed her.

But he'd also sworn to himself when Fiona had died, he'd never get close to another living soul again.

Then his eyes focused on the last few lines on the itinerary and he frowned at Nicole. 'What have you done!'

# Fifteen

Her body ached, leg muscles burned, and her hair was damp from the morning dew. Yet, she was delighted to be here, even if she was suffering on the steepest final climb, it was Mount Sonder. Panting for breath, she admired the sweet scent of sunrise mixed with the taste of red dust.

She wished Brett was here to push her.

Like every morning and night, she'd wished he was there with her, to talk to her, or to just share that comfortable silence walking side by side.

But she'd always planned to do this on her own.

Yet, she'd never been truly alone. Having walked

amongst a group she'd met as strangers, they'd become friends after sharing six days of sweat, muscle aches and consistent fly swatting, following blue arrows that marked the red dusty trail ahead.

She'd shivered through icy morning frosts that stiffened bones and clothes. Sweltered as the noon-day desert dust covered her boots that crunched upon ochre rocks made from towering jagged mountains.

She'd laughed at the antics of lizards frolicking upon the rocks, and was envious of brush-tailed rock wallabies that leaped across boulders like springboards.

They'd discovered secluded waterholes where gum trees reflected off the glistening oasis that was perfect for swimming in the mid-winter heat. And in the cooling late afternoons their pitched tents were always a welcoming sight, promising a good night's sleep.

It was there, preparing for her shower, she'd smile at Brett's notes of encouragement, discovered in her pack rolled within her clean clothes. Another note to add to the ones she already kept close to her heart.

She couldn't wait to tell him about the distant dingos that serenaded fiery desert sunsets, or the stories shared around the campfires as camp oven aromas filled the air. Thinking of him, she'd whisper her wishes to falling stars among the billion-star skyline of silence.

Always at the back of the parade, Jessica stepped steady. She'd skinned her knees and bruised her shins. Her boots slipped on sand, and her poles got trapped between rocks. Yet, every time she tripped, she'd hear Brett telling her to *get up, dust yourself off, and keep moving forward*. And she would, missing him more.

She'd been a fool to leave him behind.

Jessica had begun this final climb from three this morning, scrabbling over rocks like ants on the track in the dark. She'd been grateful to all those morning walks in the winter darkness with Brett's headlamp he'd given her, that she now wore with pride, stepping with surety.

Her reward for all that effort—an endless view.

Dumping her pack onto the red dirt, she let go of her poles and stood tall, on her own, completely unaided, and raised her fists to the sky. She'd made it.

Her heart pounded and she raised her face to greet the sunrise and had never held more inner pride until that moment.

She'd done it.

Standing tall, Jessica stared at the magnormous view before her, it was the bigger picture and she was nothing more than a speck on the wold's landscape spread vastly before her.

She knew deep within her soul she was going to be perfectly capable of achieving anything she wanted in her future.

It was then her inner voice was silenced and all her fears were still, and she just drank in the view of the MacDonald Ranges. The peaks and troughs of the land rolled out before her like an open ocean of golden russet waves trapped in mid-motion. It kissed a cerulean skyline, where a lone eagle's stretched winged glide greeted the day.

It was purely magical.

And again, Jessica wished Brett was here to share it with her. He'd appreciate it.

She'd reached her goal.

And now she knew what she wanted to do!

'You did it.'

'Brett?' She spun towards the familiar voice and swiped at the dirt around her eyes. 'Am I hallucinating?'

'No.' Chuckling, Brett hugged her warmly.

'What are you doing here?' She inhaled his familiar scent deep into her lungs, his heartbeat strong beneath her palm.

'I've been waiting here to shake your hand.'

'Huh?' She stared, mouth open as he shook her hand, giving her that easy side-grin that filled her chest with warmth.

'Congratulations.'

'Stuff the handshake.' She threw her arms around his strong shoulders as the words spilled before she could stop them. 'I've missed you so much.'

'I missed you too.'

His safe embrace made her body aches disappear. But did she hear right? He missed her? 'How did you get here?'

'Nicole saw how upset I was. She had a chat with Maggie, who booked my flights and organised everything. They even got Bob to look after the farm for me.'

'Why?'

'I've been waiting for you, hoping you'll be okay with what I have to tell you.'

'Tell me what?'

'I love you, Jessica, and I want to take you home with me.'

'You do?' Her eyes widened at this male-mirage.

'Yes. And I know you love me too.'

She whimpered, 'But—'

'Don't you dare believe your leg is an issue. Not after this. You did this trip on your own.'

'I had help. These people helped me, and you did too because you were with me every step of the way.' She showed him all his notes she kept in her pocket close to her heart.

Brett stepped closer, his callused palm encased her hand between their chests, and with their noses barely apart, he said, 'Everyone needs help, like you've helped me, too. Just seeing your smile is worth being by your side, especially when you achieve your goals.'

'I know now why I could never see beyond this,' she said, waving her other hand to the vista below them. 'I get why I haven't been able to plan a future.' It consumed her entire heart that seemed to beat for only one. 'It's you, Brett,' she said, cupping his cheek. 'There is no future without you, except for the one we can plan together.'

'Do you really mean that?'

'Yes.' Tears started to blur her vision. 'Absolutely. If you didn't show up, I was going to find you, hoping you'll agree to plan our future together?'

'You can count me in on that deal. I swear your smile just got brighter.'

'I can't stop smiling now you're here. A year ago, today, was the—'

'Stop.' His thumb pressed lightly against her lips and she stared deeply into his delicious denim eyes. 'Let's remember today as the beginning of our journey for a new life, because I won't delay living my life without you for another second.'

Wiping at the streaming tears mixing with the red dust sprinkled over her cheeks. 'I must be dreaming this?'

'Let's make it a good dream then.' He leaned closer and captured her lips with his and the whole world dropped away to only hold Brett and her.

As the sun chased away the night's shadows of yesterday, she allowed herself to believe in today and their many shared tomorrows as part of their new life. And she truly believed it. 'I love you too, Brett.'

'Don't ever stop telling me and I'll never stop walking beside you. Don't you dare leave me behind again.'

'I won't. Don't you leave me stranded in the dark

either?'

'I won't, because I want to be there to catch you so you'll never fall.'

And she believed him as her heart opened to become as light as the feather of a migrating bird that had headed north to find where her heart truly belonged — with him. 'Now can we go have a hot shower and lay in bed for a few days and order room service? Maybe have a massage too?' She murmured, leaning against him, admiring his outdoorsy male aroma, up close and personal.

'Deal.' He shared that easy grin, kissing her cheek that ached from smiling. 'Before we do, let's take a photo of this moment as the first day our future began.' With their arms wrapped around each other, the phone's camera captured their wide smiles while the world spread endlessly beneath their boots.

Jessica found her happiness, herself, and her soulmate, in the heart of the country, and she knew her next destination was Heart Springs that would become her home with Brett.

Forever.

# The ART of
# Dust

## MEL A ROWE

# One

It's a strange sensation being weighed down by guilt. It made Kat grip the steering wheel tighter while her internals stirred with the giddy sensation she'd once loved as a child. All from the faded road sign that read, *Welcome to Elsie Creek.*

'Did you live here, Mummy?' Kaytlyn asked, brushing away the auburn strands freeing themselves from her pigtails. Her sparkling, lapis lazuli blue eyes, took in the passing view.

'Only for the summers.'

'When?' Kaytlyn asked, straining her neck to see while her finger marked the page of the colouring book nestled within her purple tutu.

'Before you were born.' Back when life was so much simpler.

'How come you've never told me about this place?'

Kat never wanted to. She didn't even want to make this trip.

'Is that a tractor? And, it's...*moving.*' Kaytlyn waved energetically at the farmer like he was a famous movie star, driving a slow tractor as they passed him on the road. 'This is the country, isn't it? Like real milk-making country?'

'Not that kind of cow, sweetheart. They're beef cattle.'

Their hire van, with the U-Haul trailer rattling behind them, slowed as they approached the herd spilling over the sides of the road. Men in sweat-stained Akubra's steered their quads around the cattle with horns bigger than the handlebars on their bikes. Stocky Blue and Red Heelers yapped at the Brahman's heels, while more stockmen on horseback whistled as the odd stockwhip crack rang in the air.

'Mum, they're cowboys rounding up the herd!'

'Don't call them that. This is Australia and they're cattlemen, stockmen, ringers or drovers, and they're mustering the mob or they're droving. *I think* — it's been a while.'

She drove through the herd and continued along the open highway that stretched like a never-ending black carpet. It sliced through the centre of red dirt scrublands, with the railway line running alongside. All heading for the tiny Northern Territory town, dead ahead.

They passed rolling fields of drying grass waving in the breeze like a huge green sea. Tall gum trees crested hills that kissed the cerulean skyline where wallabies lazed in their shade. Nestled amongst its bark-peeling branches were flocks of white cockatoos, hiding from the late afternoon sun. The familiar countryside generated an electrical hum beneath Kat's skin. She was glad this long drive was almost over.

Then the hard part would begin.

Again, the weight of dread slammed heavily across her shoulder blades.

'Can't wait to go bushwalking with you, Mummy.' Kaytlyn clicked the heels of her new hiking boots, peeking out from the edge of her tutu.

Kat hadn't hiked in years. 'Tell me again, please, what are the rules of walking anywhere out here?'

'Always take a hat, a water bottle, sunscreen, snacks for the trail, and tell someone where you're going. Carry a big stick to smack the ground to scare snakes and goannas getting suntans across the tracks. Don't use the stick to poke down holes, coz the scorpions and spiders can kill you. Don't climb trees that don't have green ants on 'em coz they'll have white ants that eat trees inside out, so they'll break. Don't play near fruit bats coz they can make you very, very sick. Don't pat the cattle coz of their horns…um, am I missing something?'

'Water. What did I tell you about the water? It's the most important,' —*and terrifying*— 'part.'

'Oh, I'm never ever allowed to go swimming in any of the water holes, billabongs, rivers, lakes, streams or seas, and I have to stay back from the water's edge coz the man-eating crocodiles like to eat children for lunch.'

The place didn't sound like fun at all. 'Are you okay with all that?' Kat wasn't.

'I can't wait. How come you know all this when you grew up in the city, like me?' Kaytlyn sat taller, her fingertips reaching for the dashboard, causing her crayons to spill out of her tutu and onto the floor of their rental van.

'I used to stay with Uncle Frank and Aunty Bea for school holidays.' A time she once lived for.

'Bee, like a black and yellow stripy bee that stings? I can spell that—B.E.E.'

'Brilliant. Although, the native bees here don't sting, but the wasps do.' Was there anything good she could share without scaring her daughter back to the more civilized southern states of Australia. 'Oh, and you spell Aunty Bea, B.E.A. It's short for Beatrice.'

Kaytlyn sat back mouthing the letters, committing the new spelling word to her fast-growing vocabulary. 'How come they don't visit us?'

'How many days has it taken us to get here?'

'Five. It's the longest road trip of my life!'

Kat laughed at the seriousness of the six-year-old wearing a tutu and hiking boots.

'Do Aunty Bea and Uncle...' Kaytlyn waved her crayon like a wand.

'Frank, short for Franklin.' Everyone's name was shortened, including her own of Kathryn to Kat.

'Yeah, him. Do they have any children I can play with?'

'No.' *They would've loved some.* 'I'm sure there are

plenty of new friends to make in your new school, honey.' Kat hoped she sounded excited when she'd rather be back in their studio apartment. All this space was daunting compared to the comforting claustrophobic cocoon of a capital city.

She sat higher behind the steering wheel as they entered the town's main street, with its row of shops on either side. There was the hardware-feedstore, the small supermarket, and the mighty pub that stood proud as the centre of this small country town. There was a park with signs pointing to the train station's Tea Room.

Even though she hadn't seen the place in seven years, the town was the same, as if stuck in some weird time warp, except now it had a set of pedestrian lights guarding a zebra crossing.

'What's that?' Kaytlyn asked, pointing to the road ahead.

Kat slammed on the brakes and stared over the steering wheel with wide eyes. 'I think it's a water buffalo.'

A short, black, shiny-nosed water buffalo stood smack in the middle of the road, in the centre of town. It stared at them through long black lashes, chewing like a cow, with red ribbons waving on the breeze from its curved horns.

Was it going to charge their hire van?

'It's got ribbons on it, Mummy, so it must be someone's pet, huh?'

A ute across the road tooted its horn, and the driver shouted out of his window. '*Get off the road, Cecil.*'

The buffalo kept chewing as he ever so casually strolled in front of Kat's car. Red ribbons waved off its horns and tail, and on its sides were large letters written in bright red chalk.

'What does that writing say, Mummy?'

'Um…Choose your movie for the marathon today.'

*Weird.*

As the buffalo ambled along the sidewalk, they continued down the main street in silence. At the outer edge of town, they turned onto a bitumen road, where properties extended into acreage.

A group of children played in the street while push bikes lay in the grass on the side of the road.

Déjà vu hit Kat like she'd woken inside a dream,

slowing down for the game of street-cricket where the children stopped and stared as they drove past.

'Mummy, how come they're playing on the road?'

'They do that in the country.' Just like she used to.

'There are more children on this street than in our whole building. Will they all be going to my new school?'

'I assume so.' There was only one local bush school, with the nearest boarding school over four hours away by bus. It was a ride Kat knew well.

They approached the road's dead-end before an expansive field of golden grasses that rippled in the breeze. At the sight of the two-storey weather-worn house, her heart hitched a lump into her throat. 'We're here.'

# Find the rest of the story
at your favourite online bookstore...

or at

# MELAROWE.COM

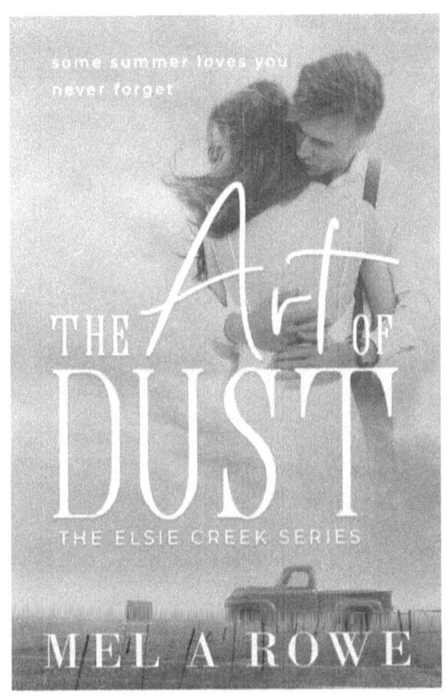

# Don't miss out

on your next

## *ESCAPE* TO HAPPILY EVER AFTER

*(#Escape2HEA)*

Join Mel A ROWE's vibrant email group

for local-lingo definitions, updates, specials

& insights on NEW RELEASES at

https://melarowe.com/newsletter/

Go on, you deserve to be spoiled.

# ABOUT THE AUTHOR

Australian Bestselling Author, Mel A ROWE, creates escapes for you to enjoy from the comfort of home.

Delivered with a dash of drama, witty humour and quirky family units, Mel is known for reinventing romantic versions of *home*, taking her common characters on uncommon journeys that lead from boardrooms to billabongs as they try to find their own HAPPILY EVER AFTER.

Living in Northern Australia, Mel enjoys random outback road trips, fumbling with her camera, annoying her family with her bad singing, and making new friends in the middle of nowhere—except for water buffalos. She's been chased by a few.

Feel free to contact Mel as her word journey continues at…

## MelAROWE.com

# ACKNOWLEDGEMENTS

Thank you for reading this story.

Thank you to the Handbrake for not disowning me, and to my sister for supporting me. Even though neither of you have ever read anything I've written, I'm leaving this right here in case you do.

Thank you to Renee Conoulty on the other side of Australia, and to the amazing Heather Warmboldt on the other side of the planet. This story would not have been possible without your help.

Thank you to my *Fabulous First Readers* team, I'm blessed to have you join me in my writing journey. Your support is priceless.

Lastly, to you, dear reader, again I thank you for taking the time to read this novella, and I look forward to sharing more with you in that *Escape to Happily Ever After*

Thank you, because I can, because I did, and because I continue to be eternally grateful …

Until next time,

A. ROWE

If you loved this story, why not let other fabulous readers like yourself find me, by sharing your book review at your favourite online bookstore, GOODREADS, or BOOKBUB